ONE LAST KISS

*The Knights of Berwyck: A Quest Through Time,
Book Five*

SHERRY EWING

Kingsburg Press
P.O. Box 475146
San Francisco, CA 94147
www.kingsburgpress.com

Front Cover Design: SelfPubBookCovers.com/lisa.messegee
Back Cover Design: Claudia Bost at www.designsbycwb.com

One Last Kiss/Sherry Ewing -- 1st ed.
ISBN eBook: 978-1-946177-93-3
ISBN Print: 978-1-946177-92-6
Library of Congress Control Number: 2019907624

A Kiss for Charity

The Earl Takes A Wife within ***Valentines From Bath***

a Bluestocking Belles Collection 2019

Nothing But Time, *A Family of Worth: Book One*

One Moment In Time*: A Family of Worth, Book Two*

Under the Mistletoe

Join Sherry's newsletter at http://bit.ly/2vGrqQM

www.SherryEwing.com

ONE LAST KISS

DEDICATION

For my friend Sarah M...

Thank you for your friendship and for the laughs when I need them the most. This ones for you, Sarah. I think you'll get a kick out of Chapter Nine!

PROLOGUE

Scotland, Lennox Castle
The Year of Our Lord's Grace 1164

Thomas of Clan Kincaid stood afore a fire in the hearth of his father's solar, but nothing could penetrate the chill running through his body. He had been in this exact same spot more times in his youth than could be counted. But *this... this* was different.

His father would not be lenient with his latest offense. He would take this as a direct insult to the entire clan. He brushed his hand over his eyes as though such an act would erase the memories of what his rash act would most likely cost him.

Was it only yester morn that his sire had at last thought Thomas old enough to take possession of a relic that had been passed down through the genera-tions, always to the oldest son of the Kincaid clan? His father had woven the tale for years: how their Viking ancestors had forged a ring of gold, a guiding star gracing the center like a compass leading the bearer to his heart's desire—a woman to share his life. Thomas had scoffed at such romantic gibberish. His only desire was to know his father thought him responsible enough to now take over the treasure. At ten and four summers, was he not a man?

He moved to a window and looked over the forest, the damned woods having been the place where life as he had known it had surely ended. When his father had given him the ring, he had appeared so proud, something Thomas rarely saw. How he had beamed to be at the receiving end of such a look. But finding himself wrapped in his father's fierce embrace had caught Thomas off guard. His sire had grumbled something incoherent afore sending his son on his way. Thomas could have sworn those whispered words were *I love you* and only now began to wonder if this would be the one and only time he would hear such sentiment from his father.

Happiness had overwhelmed Thomas when he relived the memory of placing the ring in a pouch upon his belt. He had felt as though he had stood a little taller when he had left his sire's solar and made his way out of the keep and through the outer bailey 'til he reached the stables. He had sent a lad to saddle his horse and in no time was vaulting onto his steed. With a squeeze of his legs, he put the animal into motion and raced through the woods.

Thomas had ridden for miles afore he at last halted his steed upon a rise. 'Twas there he could see just the top of the battlement walls of Lennox Castle. 'Twould be his one day, along with leading the clan once his sire passed. He had taken out the ring, staring down upon the symbol that meant he was a man in his father's eyes. He slipped it upon his finger...

...and promptly fell off his horse as a vision of a woman swam afore his eyes. Long blonde hair swayed in the breeze whilst she sat on the sandy seashore as boats with sails swept the vessels along the water's waves. An orange bridge, the likes of which Thomas had never seen afore, had strange creatures scurrying across the span, but for the life of him, he had no idea what they were.

Thomas continued to witness the scene as though he stood right behind this strangely clad woman, who began scrunching her toes in the sand. She reached down to brush off an object she had found near her hand. Inspecting it for several moments, she flinched as though she sensed something. She finally turned, holding out the object for him to take. If seeing the exact ring he now held in his hands was not enough, then the sight of her bright green eyes had Thomas reaching for the ring upon his hand.

"Sorcery," he had yelled out. Afore he had known what was happening, he had come out of his trance-like state when he pulled the ring from his finger and flung it away from him.

Horror had consumed him as he had watched the ring his father had so recently entrusted to him disappear far below. He jumped onto his horse and headed in the direction he thought the ring had landed. Hours had he searched, even returning this very morn to take up his search, but 'twas of no use. The ring was gone.

The door opened, pulling Thomas out of his memories of the day afore and into his worst nightmare. He squared his shoulders to face his sire and the tirade he knew was coming. The smile faded from his father's face as their eyes met. Perchance he saw the loss in Thomas's own.

"What have ye done now?" His father was never one to put off the inevitable. 'Twas what made him a laird to be reckoned with or feared among neighboring clans.

There was no sense trying to delay his punishment. "I lost it."

His father's fists tightened at his sides. He opened and closed his mouth several times afore he was able to speak. "The ring?" he growled out between clenched teeth.

Thomas bowed his head. "Aye, Father, but I can explain..." A gut-wrenching howl emerged from his father's throat.

"Explain? How the devil do ye think ye can explain the loss of something so vital tae our clan?" His father's wrath practically shook the rafters, which showered dust on Thomas's head.

"'Twas bewitched, Father," he attempted to explain. "I put the ring on and had visions of—"

"Enough!" His father shook his fist in the air afore his shoulders slumped in defeat. "I swore tae yer mother ye needed greater wisdom afore ye took the responsibility of such a treasure, but she convinced me otherwise. Ye have disappointed me for the last time."

"Please listen tae me, father, and try tae understand." Thomas flinched, waiting for the raised hand to land upon his cheek, but instead, his father swore again afore he went to his desk to take out parchment and quill. "What are ye doing?" Thomas squeaked out.

His father did not answer but continued to scratch away with the quill. Thomas had a sinking feeling whatever his father was writing would be determining his fate. The scowl deepened across his father's brow. He never once wavered, even whilst he dripped hot wax upon the missive and sealed it.

"From this day forward, I disown ye and no longer claim ye as my son," his father declared, a grim line of displeasure creasing his mouth. He did not look at Thomas but instead, gazed out the window.

"Father, please!" Thomas cried out, falling to his knees. Mayhap if he begged, his father would change his mind. Thomas was unprepared for the words that came tumbling out of his father's mouth next.

"I have written tae a distant relative of yer mother's asking Douglas of Clan MacLaren tae take ye in."

"Ye canna send me away! Not like this. Please forgive me, Father," he pleaded as fear ripped across his chest with thoughts of being disowned and forbidden to ever return home. Knowing his sire as he did, Thomas should not have been surprised when the man turned his back to his son to grasp at the shutter with white knuckles. No mercy would be given this day.

"Henceforth, ye are no longer welcome here. Ye best get tae packing yer bags and say yer farewell tae yer mother. A guard will escort ye tae Berwyck. I never wish tae see ye again. Now leave me!"

A childlike cry was torn from Thomas's lips when he burst from the solar to seek out his room. If he did not hurry, his sire would no doubt send someone to force him from the keep whether he was packed or not. He went to the chest at the foot of his bed and began throwing his garments into a satchel as fast as he could.

But 'twas the tears from his mother as he left the grounds that would haunt Thomas for years to come. He looked back only once to engrain in his memory a home he would never see again and cursed his ancestor's ring that had cost him all he held dear.

CHAPTER 1

Present Day, Two days before Christmas
Birmingham, Michigan

J ade Calloway pulled the collar of her coat closer to her face in some useless attempt to block out the howling winter's wind. Her boots sloshed through the mush on the sidewalk as she slipped and skidded on the icy pavement. She was so tired of this weather and was beginning to wonder if she'd ever get to San Francisco for the holiday. Her plane had already been canceled once.

Jade hoped a blizzard wouldn't hit the area causing another delayed flight. She must need her head examined to be traipsing about on such a frigid night, but her friend had insisted they meet to exchange presents before her rescheduled flight in the morning. She pulled down the brim of her knit hat as she continued on her way. Glancing down at the plastic bag she carried confirmed her worse fears. She'd be lucky if the wrapping paper on the gift she brought wasn't completely ruined.

At the distant sound of screeching tires and crashing metal, Jade was glad she'd decided to walk instead of using her car. This was one of those sub-zero snowy nights, the kind that freezes your tongue to a lamppost, or a finger to a ring. Even a snowplow shouldn't be out on the roads in this kind of weather.

Reaching an intersection, she looked up to get her bearings while snowflakes attached themselves to her eyelashes. Wiping her face with her mittens, the lights of her friend's apartment building were glowing like a beacon in the distance. She crossed the street, happy she was almost to her destination. The liberally sprinkled salt on the walkway crunched as she climbed the steps to the door. Thankful she had arrived in one piece without slipping on black ice, she rang the buzzer.

"Zoe, it's me! Open up. I'm freezing," she called into the speaker.

"Come on up!" Zoe answered along with a quick squeal of excitement before the sound was cut off and the lock buzzed to allow Jade inside the building.

The heat in the entryway welcomed her like a long-lost friend. She pulled off her mittens and began unbuttoning her coat before she made for the stairway. Climbing to the second floor, she'd barely reached Zoe's apartment when the door was thrust open, like her friend knew she was about to knock.

"Hi ya, Jade. Merry Christmas!" Zoe exclaimed, wrapping Jade in a fierce hug. Her friend's apartment smelled of sage, and she wondered what evil spirits Zoe was trying to exorcise from her place. "Jade's here, everyone!"

Everyone? She had no time to satisfy her curiosity about who else was inside because Zoe quickly turned her around to face the door she had just entered and began pulling her coat from her shoulders. Jade had thought this was to be just a gathering between the two of them. She was hardly in the mood to socialize with a bunch of people.

Turning once more to face the room, she handed Zoe her scarf, along with her hat with her mittens stuffed inside. Jade almost let out a sigh of relief to find there were only two other women present. She gave them a small smile.

One woman with long black hair stood and came over to her. "Hi. I'm Bridgette," she said, introducing herself before pointing to the blonde she had been sitting with, "and this is my good friend Megan."

"Nice to meet you," Jade replied, shaking Bridgette's hand. "How do you know Zoe?"

"That's a funny story," Bridgette answered before turning back to sit on the couch next to Megan.

"There is nothing funny about how we met. It was

fate," Zoe declared, coming from the hallway where she had taken Jade's coat.

Megan half laughed, half snorted. "You threw salt over your shoulder, and it landed in my eye when I turned in my seat to get something from my purse hanging on the back of my chair," she corrected.

"I wasn't about to have bad luck by not tossing some after I tipped the salt shaker over," Zoe said, before sitting down in an overstuffed chair. "Everything happens for a reason. The planets aligned. We were destined to meet."

Jade bit back a smile and took a seat. She watched Zoe's animated face as she talked about how her crystals had foretold how she would encounter the two women that day. She looked at her friend, and Jade was reminded how Zoe always seemed like she was born in the wrong era. She would have fit in perfectly in the sixties—minus the drugs, of course.

She remembered the first time she had met Zoe at a fair. Zoe was reading tarot cards in her booth. Her reddish-brown hair had been long and straight, a circlet of flowers around her head. Seth, Jade's boyfriend at the time, thought it'd be a hoot to see in what direction their future would lead them, but Jade had been skeptical. She didn't mind people having their own beliefs, but she was more of a *seeing is believing* kind of a girl.

To appease the man, they had sat down at Zoe's table. Jade remembered having her doubts that the woman before her would tell her anything she didn't already know. Seth would break her heart. He already had once before, and she had taken him back on his promise to never cheat on her again. God, what a fool she had been.

Lost in her memories, she could still see as clear as day when Zoe had laid down the cards after shuffling them. Her soft brown eyes had appeared as though she was seeing more than whatever the cards were *saying*. She quickly gathered them back up and pushed Seth's money back across her table, mumbling something about bad karma, and she couldn't see their future. As Seth began complaining and turned to leave, Zoe had slipped Jade a business card, quietly asking her to contact her.

Jade had taken the card, hardly knowing what to think, other than her assumptions were right all along. The woman was a fraud. Still... there was something in the woman's eyes that compelled Jade to meet with Zoe at a local coffee shop several days later. She wasted little time getting straight to the point.

Zoe warned Jade that Seth's aura was nothing but bad, and she should get herself away from him before he dragged her down into a place no woman wants to go. Knowing her relationship with the man was already beginning to sour, she broke up with him the next day. One month later, Jade saw on the news he had been arrested for drug trafficking. Knowing she had dodged a bullet, Jade and Zoe had been friends ever since, even though Zoe tended to be overly superstitious about most things.

Jade was brought back from her inner thoughts when Zoe stood to light another bundle of sage, waving the herb about the room with some kind of ceremonial fanfare. With Christmas right around the corner, Jade would rather the place smell like spiced cinnamon or a fresh-cut tree decorated with bright lights and ornaments.

Zoe then came to stand before Jade's chair, taking her hand to pull her upright. She then did the same with Bridgette. "The reason I wanted you both here tonight is because I wanted the two of you to meet."

"That's all very nice, Zoe, but it could have waited until I returned from San Francisco," Jade replied, squeezing her friend's hand.

Zoe got her strange, far-off look. "You will be traveling far soon..."

"Yes... tomorrow, dear. *San Francisco*," she emphasized with a snort.

"Your lives are now linked..." Zoe murmured more like a chant than mere words spoken in a normal tone.

Jade and Bridgette exchanged glances.

Bridgette shrugged. "I'm sure we'll all become good friends," she replied in a hushed tone.

Megan moved to sit on the edge of the couch. "I'm feeling a little left out here, Zoe," she complained.

Zoe turned to Megan. "Hush! Your path and mine

do not follow the same crossroads at this point in time as Jade and Bridgette."

Megan crossed her arms over her chest. "Whatever," she pouted before snapping her lips shut and sitting back in her seat. A frown marred her face.

Zoe returned to focusing her attention on Jade and Bridgette. "Take hands," she urged.

It was now Jade's turn to shrug. "We might as well humor her," she replied, holding out her hand for Bridgette to take.

The instant their hands clasped together, a small shock of tingling sensations raced up her arm. Bridgette's eyes widened when their gazes met.

"The connection is complete," Zoe whispered, before squeezing Jade's hand and looking deeply into her eyes. "You're about to go on an incredible journey," she said before turning her gaze to Bridgette. "You will also follow soon. You both have been given a rare opportunity. It's not bad luck but karma allowing you to have your heart's desire. Do not be afraid but go with an open mind to meet your destiny. You are being given a gift. I will miss you both."

With her words sounding much like a premonition of things to come, Zoe let go of their hands, and Jade's left arm fell to her side. She and Bridgette both finally let go, but given Bridgette's frown, the other woman shared the same puzzling confusion as Jade herself was feeling.

Once seated again, the women exchanged their gifts

with Zoe and their conversation turned to what everyone would be doing for the remainder of the holiday season. Before Jade knew what was happening, everyone was being ushered out of Zoe's apartment with Merry Christmas wishes. Jade stood on the doorstep, gazing at Bridgette and Megan.

"That was super odd," Bridgette said as they began to make their way down the stairs.

Megan tossed her scarf over her shoulder before opening the building door and walking along the sidewalk. "I know she's a bit strange, and she's our friend and all, but that whole *thing* upstairs kind of creeped me out."

Jade pulled her mittens on. "Zoe is who she is, and nothing will change her." As they reached the intersection, they all stopped. "I'm heading that way," Jade said, pointing across the street.

Bridgette nodded in the opposite direction. "We're going this way. Guess we'll be seeing you around. Nice meeting you."

"Same here. See ya," Jade replied as she watched them cross the street with a wave goodbye.

It was only when Jade was in the comfort of her own home that she ran through what happened in Zoe's apartment. A laugh escaped her. At twenty-six, she was too old to believe in magic. Thinking only of her trip in the morning, she went to sleep dreaming of San Francisco and what excitement the city by the bay might bring.

CHAPTER 2

Berwyck Castle,
Winter, The Year of Our Lord's Grace 1182

Thomas, lately of Berwyck, grabbed at the cloak threatening to leave his body whilst the wind whipped all around him. The ground was blanketed with a fine layer of snow, and yet he knew this was only the beginning of the storm to come.

For nigh unto ten and eight years, he had served at Berwyck Castle. When he had arrived, he had been put under the watchful eye of the lady of the keep. Lady Catherine, who was English, had been good to him when he had shown up at the barbican gate. She had treated him as part of her family, even going so far as to see he had his own chamber within the keep. He had been grateful for her to extend such a courtesy to a distant relation.

Thomas could almost still see himself as the young tormented lad of ten and four summers who mourned the loss of all he had known. He had plunged himself into mimicking Lady Catherine's accent 'til he had perfected an English drawl in the hope of forgetting his past... not that he ever could.

But living at a castle located on the border between Scotland and England hardly allowed for Thomas to forget his origins, not when the MacLaren clan ruled Berwyck Castle. He had soon begun his training with Laird Douglas and his men. After several years, he had then been appointed an honored guardsman to the eldest daughter, Lady Amiria, who was now Berwyck's mistress. He still mourned the loss of Lady Catherine who had met an early demise with the birth of her last child, Patrick.

He shook his head as memories of the long, bloody siege assailed his head from years long past. Lady Amiria had been forced to hide in disguise as her twin brother Aiden. She eventually fell in love with the very enemy who now was Thomas's liege lord. Dristan, who had a reputation of being the Devil's Dragon, was a fair lord, and Thomas had no issue continuing his service once the knight claimed the land in the name of King Henry II. But those were still troubled times, at least to some, and when Lady Amiria's affection went to the new lord in charge of Berwyck, Thomas had followed Ian, who had once been Lady Amiria's captain of the guard and had apparently been in love with her.

Someone had to protect his back, and it might as well be Thomas.

They had traveled near and far, hiring out their swords or entering tourneys for a bit of coin. They had even traveled to Edinburgh in Scotland. The city was so close to what Thomas used to call home that it pained him to know he was but a few miles from Lennox Castle. Yet he said nothing, and when fate changed the course of Ian's life, they returned to Berwyck where Thomas decided to stay. There was nothing left for him to return to at his place of birth. Now at a score and twelve, he was old enough to realize his father's lack of faith in him had ensured there was no reason to return.

Thomas hesitated whilst continuing his way through the inner bailey. With a brief glance at the chapel, he decided against attending evening Mass and instead made his way to the keep. The heavy door boomed as he swung it shut. The room was eerily silent as he moved toward the fire in the Great Hall to warm himself. He had missed yet another Mass, but for some reason, he was restless of late. Sitting for hours at his prayers would give him no comfort this night, and he knew Father Donovan would surely take him to task when their paths crossed on the morrow, most likely with extra time afore the altar on his knees. His stomach rumbled, giving testament he had, at the very least, been fasting in preparation for the upcoming Christmas feast.

The keep door opened, and Thomas prepared for

the reprimand for not attending evening Mass. He was not prepared for the traveler who hurried across the floor to stand next to him by the fire.

"Greetings, Thomas," the young knight said as he stripped off his sodden gloves and held his hands out toward the fire.

"By *Saint Michael's Wings!* Aiden, what are you doing here?"

"This is still my home, is it not?"

Thomas reached over, and they clasped forearms in greeting. "You surprised me is all," he beamed in reply. "'Tis good to see you. Your sister will be pleased your feet finally followed their way home."

Aiden chuckled. "Almost did not make it with the storm," he stated, nodding toward the door.

"Where have you been?"

"Visiting Ian and my sister Lynet up at Urquhart Castle. She now has a fine bonny lassie named Genevieve. Ian is already sharpening his sword in preparation for any man who thinks he may be worthy of wedding her."

The two men laughed but had no further time to have speech afore the keep door burst open again to admit those who had been in Berwyck's chapel. The room began to fill quickly, and Lady Amiria's cry of happiness rang out once she espied her brother. The twins embraced afore they made their way to a secluded corner to carry on their own conversation.

Dristan's personal guardsmen entered the hall and

began sitting at various tables whilst those of the MacLaren clan were dispersed among them. There were always several knights training at Berwyck with the Devil's Dragon, but Thomas did not care for the men who were now present. He had seen for himself their true character on a number of occasions and was surprised his liege lord allowed them to stay. Still... for some odd reason, Thomas suddenly felt as though he did not belong here and for the first time in many a year, he wished he could return home.

Someone's hand came to gently rest upon his shoulder, and he turned to stare down into the green eyes of Kenna, Berwyck's healer and wife to Dristan's guardsman, Geoffrey. Although she appeared as though she was seeing him, Thomas could tell she was witnessing what only God himself knew for sure. Kenna had visions from time to time, and although he had gotten used to hearing her predict some knight's futures, he preferred to keep himself away from the woman. Her *gift* was too reminiscent of his own strange happening when he had touched that damned ring in his youth. He would not think on the other happenings of women from other places in time finding their way to Berwyck.

Kenna suddenly swayed, and Thomas reached out to catch her. "Geoffrey!" he called out and was surprised when the woman tightly gripped her fingers around his wrist.

"She is coming soon" she gasped out.

Thomas frowned. "Who?"

Kenna's eyes rolled upward, and Thomas feared she was seeing more of his future than he would want to learn about.

"She comes from afar... but know she is here for you and you alone. Take care to protect her," she urged afore she once more looked upon Thomas with clear eyes. She smiled as though she was giving him a most prized gift he should cherish.

Afore he knew what to make of her ramblings, Geoffrey took his wife in his arms and carried her away to seek their chamber. Thomas could only stand there, stunned, for he knew not what to make of her words.

Instead of joining the company in the Great Hall, Thomas climbed the turret stairs to seek his own chamber. He rested his sword against the wall, stoked the fire, and then tumbled upon the coverlet of the bed, not even bothering to undress. And when he dreamed, he had visions of the blonde lady from long ago, sitting in the sand and holding out his family's ring for him to take.

Jade looked up at one of the towers of the Golden Gate Bridge. It was such an incredible structure, spanning two spits of land with the ocean and bay far beneath. She scanned the view before her. Standing on the roof of Fort Point afforded quite a view of the city of San Francisco, Alcatraz, and Angel Island. It was a beautiful city and so different from Michigan that Jade momentarily considered moving here.

Such a fleeting thought quickly left her mind as she slowly made her way down one of the turret stairways. She would be more alone here than she ever was back home, and at least there, she had a few people she considered friends. Good grief. She was starting to feel sorry for herself that she had no family to share the holiday with. *This is no time for a pity party, Jade.* She had saved for months to afford this trip, and she was damn well going to enjoy herself!

She left the fort, smiling and thanking the Park Service ranger who stood at the entrance. She had walked farther than she intended when she started out this morning from Pier Thirty-Nine. The entrance to the pier had been decorated for the holiday with a towering tree just waiting for night to fall so the brilliance of its lights would shine for all to enjoy. Throngs of people flooded the pier, all out to enjoy their vacations. Artists lined the walkways selling their wares while others performed for a tip or two.

It was a crazy experience, and although Jade had enjoyed all the touristy things to do and see, she had kept walking until she ended up at the fort and the end of the trail. A sign with handprints on the fence more or less told anyone who had ventured this far that they had reached it. She smiled when the joggers ran up to slap their hands upon the sign before turning right around and going back the way they had come.

Jade continued her walk along the pathway of Chrissy Field. The nearby sandy beach seemed to call to her, and since she had purposely *planned* to have no schedule, she had all the time in the world to explore the beach. Kicking off her shoes, she began making her way over the stretch of sand that felt oddly warm given the time of year. Strange how the place now seemed deserted, compared to when she passed by an hour ago.

She finally laid down her jacket and sat. Sailboats skimmed across the water, and her eyes took in the scenic view of the bay. She began digging her toes in the sand and enjoying what warmth was left from the day's sun as it touched her skin.

She placed her hands on the ground. Closing her eyes, she leaned her head back to relax when something cold touched one of her fingers. Looking down, she saw a metal ring next to her hand, as though the object had fallen off her finger. Picking up the golden band, the ring felt warm to the touch. She glanced around, but no one was close enough to have dropped it.

She began dusting sand off the object and was amazed to discover a star in the center, almost like a compass. The ring looked quite valuable, and she could only wonder how the heck it had just landed on her jacket. If she had found it in the sand, it would have been one thing but *this... this* was a new level of crazy.

She heard a gentle whisper growing louder inside her head, and she suddenly wondered if the ring's owner might be behind her. She looked over her shoulder and gasped aloud at the shadowy figure of a young boy who appeared behind her. Instinct alone had her holding up the ring as though he could actually seize what she offered. His expression quickly changed to one of shock. Stunned by what she was witnessing, she dropped the ring and the boy disappeared from view.

"What the hell?" she shouted before she realized her inner thoughts had been spoken out loud. If she had been standing, she would have surely found her knees buckling in shock.

A woman who was walking by looked down at her. "You okay?" she asked.

"Yes, I'm fine," Jade answered, rubbing her eyes as if she had imagined what had happened seconds ago.

The woman nodded and continued her walk, but not before Jade heard her muttering something about *crazy tourists*. Was she losing her mind? Jade didn't think so, and she once more inspected the ring lying on her jacket. She reached for it, her hand hovering above the golden object, almost to ensure something weird wasn't going to happen again. But it was nothing more than a ring, so she picked it up and put it in her pocket before returning to her hotel.

I must be jet lagged. Yes, that's it.

Once she reached her room, she fell back onto her bed and thought she'd take a short nap. That was all she needed. A little rest and she'd be good as new with no further hallucinations. She was more than ready to celebrate Christmas just as she had planned.

The man standing before her appeared so reminiscent of the ghostly youth she had envisioned at the beach that she had no doubt they were one and the same. His face was more mature, as though several years had now passed. His blackish brown hair hung to his shoulders, and a five o'clock shadow graced his cheeks and chin. Blue-gray eyes pierced her heart as though he knew her, which, of course, was impossible. He

frowned, and the scowl marred his otherwise handsome features.

"Who are you?" she gasped when she finally found her voice and began wondering if she really was, perhaps, losing her mind.

"What witchery is this that you come afore me in my dreams?" he all but growled out.

"This is my dream, you crazy ghost!"

"'Tis not your dream! You are invading mine," he said with fists clenched at his sides. One hand reached for the hilt of his sword. The sight of the blade appearing from its sheath made Jade take several steps away from this angry stranger.

She held out her hands to hold him off as though this meager effort would actually stop his progress. "Don't come any closer!"

He cursed, although she could in no way understand what he said for he did so in a language unfamiliar to her. Clearly, he came to some decision, since he returned his sword to its place at his side. He ran his fingers through his hair, and she became aware how adorable he looked with a few strands sticking straight up. His serious expression altered to one of curiosity, and the change was so significant that Jade was fascinated by his transformation.

His mesmerizing eyes began to freely roam over her entire body, causing her cheeks to flush when their eyes at last met.

"Your garments are most strange..." he said, nodding in her direction.

"Strange? What's so strange about jeans and a blouse?" she interrupted him.

"... *as is your speech,* mademoiselle," *he finished crossing his arms over his massive chest.*

A half laugh, half snort escaped her, and she swore she saw the corners of his mouth twitch as he, too, saw the humor in her reaction to his words.

She pointed up and down at his own attire. "What medieval faire have you been at?" she asked, marveling at his clothes that were pretty darn authentic right down to his shiny sword.

"Faire?" he questioned with a raised brow.

"Oh, come on," she teased. "Just look at you! You could be right off of a romance cover. Is that it? Are you one of those models who pose for book covers? If you are, I've got to find one with you on it. You're the perfect personification of a handsome medieval knight." She smiled as though she had finally figured him out.

His mouth dropped open before his lips snapped shut. "I have no notion of what you are babbling about, woman," he growled out.

"You don't have to be so rude," she said with a shake of her finger as though he were a misbehaving child.

He moved so quickly she had no time to put any distance between them. He took ahold of her wrist and began pulling her body toward his. Her reaction was immediate as she went to push him away, but the instant her palms landed on his chest, searing heat radiated and shot straight up her arms. He must have felt it too, for his eyes widened in surprise before his hand moved to her waist. She should be protesting their intimate contact, but she couldn't have even if she tried... or wanted to.

She was too stunned by what was going on in her body and her reaction to this handsome stranger. Whatever the reason, her heart seemed to draw its own life from being next to this man as it began hammering away in her chest.

"You have me at a disadvantage, my lady." His husky tone was a complete reversal from what came out of his mouth but a few seconds before. She watched when his lips formed a cocky grin, as though he knew exactly what she was feeling.

"I do?" she managed to whisper.

"We have met afore, have we not, and yet I know not your name. Who are you?" he asked, whispering in her ear.

Goosebumps raced down her spine as she listened to him inhale the scent of her hair.

"Y-yes, we've met, kind of. At the beach but you weren't really there. You were younger, too," she answered before hesitantly reaching up to touch his cheek. He was real!

He leaned into her palm, and her knees just about buckled.

"Who are you?" he repeated. His eyes searched hers for answers.

"Jade, and you are..." Her question trailed off but lingered in the air between them.

"Thomas," he replied, and she watched in fascination when he lowered his head, pressing his lips to her own in a gentle kiss.

CHAPTER 4

Thomas bolted upright from his bed, his fingertips automatically brushing against his mouth. His lips tingled as though they had, in truth, been kissing the woman from his dreams, a woman who was clearly not from his time. Her speech, her dress, and even the way she comported herself told him much. This woman was not some mild-mannered lady but one who was used to speaking her mind.

Rising from his bed, he tore off his tunic from the day afore and went to a chest placed in the corner of his room. His fingers shook when he lifted the lid, afore it slammed shut once more after he grabbed a fresh garment. He placed kindling on the red embers in the hearth 'til they sparked to life, yet the warmth of the growing fire did nothing to take the chill from his body. He shivered in remembrance of the same feelings from years past.

He poured a chalice of wine and sat afore the fire, lost in thought whilst staring into the flames. 'Twas not as though other strange women had not come to Berwyck's gates. Aye. Lord Dristan bitterly complained more often than not that he was losing his best knights to these future *guests* who stole the hearts of his men. In truth, he had really only lost two captains of his guard who were now happily married with children of their own. 'Twas a rare occurrence for Riorden de Deveraux or Fletcher Monroe to return to Berwyck these days. He heard tell the knights were afraid to lose their lovely ladies to *Time*.

A snort escaped Thomas whilst he pondered the mysteries of his own sorry life. His brows narrowed as he wondered if mayhap Kenna's vision was actually of one of these women from another place in time. *God's Bones*, he thought afore he drained his wine in one long gulp. How would he endure such a fate? Yet the woman in his dreams was not unfamiliar to him, and his hands again trembled as he set the now-empty chalice upon a table next to his chair.

Aye! He had seen her afore in his vision when he had first placed that infernal ring upon his finger. A ring that had cost him everything! His family, his home, and, even more importantly, his honor. Years had passed since his last petition to his father asking if he could return home. But his father still had little faith in him even after all these years, and Thomas had given in to his sire's edict that he cease attempting to contact anyone in the Kincaid clan again. 'Twas as though Thomas no longer existed as far as his sire was concerned, and he wondered, not for the first time, how his mother and siblings fared.

Enough, he shouted inside his head. 'Twould serve him no good to continue on where his mind always wandered... to return home with his honor restored in his father's eyes if he but had the ring. His lips tingled again, causing his eyes to widen. What if the woman was the key? If she, in truth, had the ring and was to travel to this time, he could petition her to give the item to him. Such an act should cost her nothing, and then Thomas could return home to where he truly belonged!

He grabbed a leather belt and fastened it afore reaching out for his sword. 'Twas the one thing he owned with the swirling design of the Kincaid clan engraved upon the gleaming metal, a grim reminder of from whence he came. He grinned with a sense of purpose afore sliding the blade into the scabbard and making his way from the room.

"Good morn, Sir Thomas," Lord Dristan announced as he fell into step with him. "Ready for a day of training?"

"My Lord," Thomas said with a short nod whilst managing to hide the groan of despair threatening to surface. A day of training in the middle of a snowstorm held no appeal. He thought of another approach. "I thought mayhap you would skip such an endeavor with Christmas but a day away."

Lord Dristan let out a deep chuckle as they began making their way down the turret stairs. "Tomorrow we shall rest, but today, we train as we do any other day. Besides, 'tis the best of days to prove your worth that you are capable of defending yourself whilst your feet threaten to slip from beneath you."

"An empty belly is hardly advantageous to a hard day's training upon the lists either, my lord."

Another laugh rumbled in Lord Dristan's chest. "I must needs have speech with the Lady Amiria. Her guardsmen are growing soft," he complained, and were it not for the twinkle in his gray eyes, Thomas would have sworn his lord was disappointed in him.

"I am not *soft*," he scoffed, "and am more than ready to prove myself at any hour of the day."

"That is the spirit, Sir Thomas," Dristan stated with a hardy slap across Thomas's shoulder.

Lord Dristan was clearly satisfied with Thomas's answer, but his lord's cheery disposition quickly turned into a mighty scowl when he witnessed a table of knights who had come to Berwyck to train with the Devil's Dragon.

They were a boisterous lot, and their leader, Gaillard de Rowen, was full of self-worth, as though God himself had shined down and bestowed upon him his talent with a sword. Thomas had not cared for the man the moment he crossed onto Berwyck's lands, and the feeling had been more than mutual.

"I will be glad when this storm abates, and I can personally toss the lot of them from my gates," Dristan growled out.

There was no need for Thomas to inquire about whom his lord was referring to. 'Twas obvious he cared not for Gaillard any more than Thomas did.

"I, too, will be happy to see them to your border, my lord. There is something about their leader that I do not care for."

Dristan's brow rose whilst he looked upon Thomas afore a smirk lit his face. "Then come. Let us see about showing Gaillard some manners and how one comports oneself under my roof."

When Dristan entered the Great Hall, he bellowed for his knights to grab their gear and report to the lists. Knights began scampering out the door as they followed his orders. Thomas's gaze met Gaillard's, and his lips curved into a cocky grin. He would show this arrogant arse a thing or two, and there was no better way than to do so with his blade in hand.

Thomas gathered his cloak around him and headed out into the storm, whistling a merry tune as he went. The day was going to be most satisfying, especially when he personally sent Gaillard sailing through the air to land in the snow. The only thing that would be better was if the woman were to appear at Berwyck with his ring.

He knew her name, and he conjured her image from his dreams. *"Jade, come back to me..."* he whispered into the winter wind in some wild hope she would in truth hear him from across the centuries keeping them apart.

CHAPTER 5

Jade reached for the man of her dreams. "Thomas!" she called out to the empty room, but the only sound was her own voice echoing his name, the name of the man whom she swore she knew. But how was that even possible? This Thomas certainly didn't live in the twenty-first century. That was *perfectly* clear! Still... she swore she could feel his lips pressed to her own. Their kiss had been but a gentle urging of what Jade knew was to come if they could have continued.

She tossed the covers from the bed and stormed to the bathroom. Plunging her head beneath the cool water of the shower should pull her out of her hallucinations. But as she washed the last of the conditioner from her hair, she turned off the water and opened the shower door to listen. She could have sworn she heard the sound of swords as they clanged together in battle.

"Get a grip on yourself, Jade. You must have turned on the television," she reprimanded herself before she grabbed a fluffy towel to dry herself and donned her clothes. Although she didn't have to worry about snow today like she would have if she had been back in Michigan, San Francisco was cold this time of year, especially with the ocean winds whipping into the bay. Her sweater and long coat should keep her warm enough while she played the tourist and explored parts of the city.

With her makeup done and her hair thrown carelessly back into a messy bun, she took only a moment to look at her reflection. She shrugged, thinking her appearance would do. Besides, she had no one to impress but herself, and that was exactly the way she wanted her vacation to be. Nothing planned, spur of the moment fun, and no drama allowed.

She grabbed her purse but dropped the brush she had planned to take with her when she left the bathroom and saw the television was turned off. Eyes wide, she listened to voices that were coming to her as clear as day. She went to the nightstand, thinking the radio was on. That, too, was off, but the ring she had left there the night before had a strange yellow glow.

"What the hell?" she cried out.

She could not seem to help herself when her hand moved forward to hover over the shiny gold metal, thinking it would be warm. She was mistaken, and she picked up the ring to look at it in her palm, finding the metal was cool to the touch. The voices grew louder until she heard the ring... No! Not the *ring*... it was *him*! She heard Thomas from her dreams!

"Jade, come back to me..."

Everything suddenly seemed as though Jade was watching some crazy sci-fi movie. How else could the ring actually be moving of its own will toward her finger even while she took hold of the shiny gold metal and attempted to pull it away with all her might?

"Someone help me," she shouted, as she continued to struggle with the ring.

Whatever magic surrounded this *thing* was way beyond Jade's ability to understand it, and she could tell she was losing the battle when the ring easily slipped onto the index finger of her left hand as though it belonged there.

She fell, or maybe, she was floating in a misty cloud of nothingness. But she was not alone, for images came to her of those whom she presumed had held the ring before her and throughout time: a Viking lord whose ancestors forged the ring's beginning; Thomas as the young boy she first saw, a ghostly apparition tossing the ring into the forest to never see it again; a man in Middle-Eastern robes showing the ring to a woman, who took it with the hand that did not cradle a baby to her breast, then handed it to a servant before the man bent to kiss her.

And still, the voices from distant times continued as images played before her while the wind whipped all around. Next came an unkempt man with his shirt open to his waist, hallucinating in an opium den before laying down the ultimate hand of cards. He looked over his winnings, mostly objects and nothing of worth except a golden ring too small for his finger. He picked up the band that was warm, almost hot to the touch, before watching in disbelief when the metal increased in size. *I need to lay off the pipe.* His words whispered inside Jade's head before she watched him slip on the ring and be slammed back into his chair with a sudden drive to return home.

Jade continued her unexpected journey until she observed the next scene. Two men, their red coats dark with rain in the glow from their campfire, sat hunched beneath a blanket in the deluge. One man reached out, offering what could only be the ring to the other, a tall, dark-haired Scot who slipped the gold band onto his finger and then gripped the hand with his other before he was lost from sight, and Jade continued onward, as though she were rushing through time itself.

The next image raced across her mind of a pale, ebony-haired, gray-eyed woman in a worn, green dress. She cradled the ring and stared out a window, dreaming of the man who'd left her. The dream was so strong, Jade instantly saw a tall man with coppery brown hair and laughing blue eyes. He wore leather pants, a flannel shirt, and a Scottish Tam. The vision faded as quickly as it had come.

The ring was once more lost until a weary-looking

young woman digging for root vegetables uncovered it in a field. Jade could hear her fanciful thoughts as the woman brushed off the ring clearly and thought the guiding star she observed might bring her to a certain man. Her laughter echoed across Jade's mind when she watched the woman place the ring in her pocket. Later, this same woman and a ginger-haired man searched the deck of a ship for the lost ring before they kissed.

Next came a man with lighter brown hair, neatly cut, who appeared to Jade as though he were a former soldier down on his luck. The scene rushed around her, and she saw the man finding the ring in the street, turning it in at a police station, only to return when no one claimed it. Time must have passed, for the next thing Jade saw was the same man and a woman sailing on a boat. The ring slipped from his finger while checking the rigging and disappeared into the dark waters below.

Everything came full circle when she saw herself finding the ring, and the image of Thomas as a grown man whispered to her in her dreams as though calling for to her to join him. *"Jade, come back to me..."*

She now found herself falling at an alarming rate of speed. Her cry for help was lost as the ring pulled her arm forward to wherever she was destined to go. Wet, cold snow stung her face until she hit the frozen ground as Thomas's name slipped easily past her lips. She looked up. There was nothing to see but whirling snow all around before her head slumped to the damp ground, and she knew no more.

CHAPTER 6

Thomas swung his sword, narrowly missing Gaillard's head when he ducked at the last instant. A satisfied smirk lit the corners of Thomas's mouth, but his smile fell when he swore he heard his name carried on the frosty wind. His opponent took his leave of the lists and ran toward the gate leading in the direction of the village. *Odd that*, Thomas thought, but even stranger was the urge to follow the knight, along with the intense feeling someone was in need of his aid.

He did not ask permission to leave but sheathed the blade at his side and followed the footprints left in the newly fallen snow. Gaillard would not earn the respect of Lord Dristan by acting the coward, and Thomas had the distinct premonition something else had caused the knight to leave the training field.

It did not take long to find out where Gaillard had gone. In truth, he had not traveled far past Berwyck's walls. Thomas observed the knight kneeling down at a fallen figure lying prone in the snow. The knight jumped to his feet and whirled around afore drawing his sword and pointing it toward Thomas.

"I claim this woman as my own," Gaillard shouted, whilst swinging his blade back and forth as though to prove his point.

Thomas came forward for he feared nothing, including the knight threatening him. He crossed his arms over his chest as though Gaillard's words held no worth. "This is not a time of war. You cannot claim some woman you just found in the snow. If she is not the wife of one of the villagers, then Lord Dristan would be bound to protect her since she has been found on his lands."

A frown crossed Gaillard's brow as he pondered Thomas's words. "She is mine," he yelled, "and not you nor the Devil's Dragon will take her from me!"

As though Gaillard's words had conjured up the man himself, Lord Dristan appeared through the falling snow. "What goes on here, and why have the two of you left the training?"

Thomas bowed. "It appears there is a woman here who is in need of our protection, my lord."

Dristan came forward to kneel down at the woman upon the ground. "I see..." he remarked, continuing his inspection.

Gaillard at last found his voice. "Lord Dristan, I claim—"

Dristan stood to peer down upon the knight afore him. "You claim nothing on my lands," he warned. "Sir Thomas, come and take this woman up to the castle. We will call for Kenna's aid and the Lady Amiria."

Satisfied the situation was now in control with his lord's appearance, Thomas came to pick up the woman. Gaillard leaned in to whisper in his ear whilst he carefully cradled the lady in his arms.

"This is not finished," Gaillard hissed with clenched teeth.

Thomas peered at Gaillard whilst he heard Dristan telling him to hurry. He looked down into the angry eyes of the knight whom he disliked even more now that he was attempting to claim someone who did not belong to him.

He gave a short laugh. "Aye, 'tis finished if you have any sense in your head," Thomas threatened.

He did not wait for a reply but carefully began making his way to the castle. Servants were scurrying up the stairs to ready a chamber for the woman. Her soft moan caused Thomas to hold her even tighter as he made his way up the turret stairs.

Lady Amiria stood at one of the bedchamber doors, holding it open for him to enter. "Quickly, Thomas, bring her inside so Kenna can see to any injuries she might have."

Thomas did as he was bid and at last laid the woman upon the coverlet of the bed. He watched in fascination when her blonde hair spilled upon the pillow 'til Thomas moved the tresses hiding her face.

His eyes widened when he at last recognized the woman who had haunted his dreams since he was a young lad. Her eyelids fluttered open, and a smile etched itself across her visage, but 'twas those mesmerizing green eyes that left Thomas speechless.

"Thomas..." She said his name like a gentle caress, striking a chord in his heart that he could not deny even if he wanted to.

"Jade," he replied, taking ahold of her hand. "You are safe."

"I knew you would find me..." Her voice trailed off as she once more closed her eyes.

Thomas stood, completely stunned afore his gaze turned to Kenna, who only gave him a brief nod. She then began ushering him from the chamber.

"Your lady is in good hands, Sir Thomas," Kenna stated with another kindly smile.

"I should stay," he attempted, only to have Lady Amiria come forward, pushing him toward the door.

"I think not, but you may check on her later. I am certain she will have as many questions as you no doubt have yourself," Amiria ordered.

And that was how Thomas found himself outside in the passageway standing by a door being firmly shut in his face. He paced the corridor, his mind full of questions only the woman inside possibly had the answer to.

Or did she? For perchance, this whole situation was far bigger than anyone could have ever imagined.

❦

Jade bolted up in her bed. "Thomas," she called out with a sense of *déjà vu*. Her eyes quickly scanned an unfamiliar bedroom until she saw two women, one with hair as black as the midnight skies and the other red as the fire they sat beside.

"Praise God, you are awake," the red-haired woman said before turning toward the other woman. "I will let the men know she has risen."

Jade had no time to question her because the woman slipped through a door. Her breathing quickened as she noticed the room had walls of stone. This was certainly not her hotel room, and Jade began to panic when the black-haired lady dressed in medieval garb came to the bedside. She perched herself on the edge and offered Jade a calming smile.

"Ye must have many a question, Jade," the woman said with a light Scottish accent. "First, my name is Kenna."

"How do you know who I am?" Jade croaked out, uncertain of what the hell was going on.

"I know many things, whether I wish it or not," Kenna replied. "Can ye tell me what ye last remember of yer journey here?"

She began searching her memory of what had

happened and recalled the ring on her finger. She gasped and tried to remove the metal, but it remained in place. Jade frowned. This was certainly odd as she could move the ring easily around her finger. Why couldn't she get this blasted ring off? It wasn't like the thing was stuck because it was too small for her finger. She swallowed hard before looking into Kenna's green eyes, so similar to her own.

"I saw... people throughout time..."

"Aye. What else?"

A vision of a dark-haired warrior with searching blue-gray eyes came to her mind. "Thomas... is he here?"

Kenna's smile broadened. "Aye, he is, and most concerned for yer welfare, I might add. Do ye not also wish tae know where ye are?"

Jade scratched at her temple. "I felt as though I was falling."

"Aye, and fall ye did. Slipping through time as some of the women afore ye have also done."

Jade laughed. "That's completely impossible."

"Is it?" Kenna went back to the fire to plunge an iron rod into the red-hot coals while she poured something into a cup. "Tell me... how does Zoe fare?"

Jade sat straight up in the bed. "You know my friend?" she asked, thinking this was all some kind of a stupid joke.

"Not in the conventional way, I suppose." Kenna took the iron from the fire and plunged it into the cup. The room began to fill with the smell of spiced wine.

"You're not answering my question. How do you know Zoe?"

"I do not know of her physically, but she is my great granddaughter... or will be someday, many generations from now."

A laugh escaped Jade's lips as she sat back upon the pillows of the bed. "Now I know you're trying to pull something over on me. Why are you and Zoe making fun of me?"

Kenna came back to the bed and offered her the cup. Jade reached out hesitantly for the goblet to sniff the contents. Wine on an empty stomach was never a good idea. Besides, how was she to know she hadn't been drugged, given the hallucinations crossing her mind?

Kenna chuckled. "We are not poisoning ye, Jade, and only have yer best interest at heart."

"How do you know what I'm thinking?"

Kenna shrugged. "I see many things, including my granddaughter having speech with ye in yer future world."

"Go on," Jade urged, wondering what other tall tale this woman would weave for her amusement.

"Ye shall learn all there is in good time, my dear, but fear not. Ye are safe here at Berwyck Castle and under the protection of Laird Dristan. Do not listen tae the serfs who gossip about him. Most of their tales are but stories tae scare those into submission who would fight against him."

Jade took a sip from the cup and found the mulled wine soothing. "Berwyck Castle? Fighting? You sound as though I'm stuck in some medieval stronghold with a siege at the gates." She took another sip, thinking of the foolish notion of her traveling through time.

"We have not had a siege upon Laird Dristan's lands for many a year, praise be tae God. Our liege lord shall keep ye safe, as will Sir Thomas."

Jade looked upon Kenna, who appeared as sane as the next person. "Just where the hell am I?" she asked, placing the cup to her lips.

"As I have told ye afore, ye are at Berwyck Castle that is situated on the border of England and Scotland. I suppose the castle's location is not necessarily important tae this conversation, but I have not told ye *when* ye are."

"*When?* I'm pretty darn sure I know what year it is. I don't feel like I hit my head." She tested her theory by running her fingers across her scalp. Nope, no signs of a bump to her noggin.

"Aye, *when*," Kenna continued in a kind tone. "Dearest Jade, ye are in the year of Our Lord's Grace 1182. In fact, ye are just in time to celebrate Christmas with the MacLaren clan and Laird Dristan's knights."

Wine spewed forth from Jade's mouth as the cup tumbled from her hands to land on the stone floor. The remaining contents drained from the goblet to leave a red trail as the cup rolled toward the hearth. Jade had no words, nor could any sound pass her lips, especially when the door slammed open, and the man from her dreams stepped through the portal. Good Lord! It was *him!*

CHAPTER 7

Thomas stared in disbelief at the terrified woman upon the bed. He turned a frown at Kenna, knowing the woman most likely was telling Jade more than she was ready to hear. *God's Wounds!* Even Thomas was having a hard time accepting the truth she was really here.

"Leave us," he ordered Kenna. "I must needs have speech with the lady."

Kenna rose, picked up her satchel of herbs from upon a table, and came to stand afore him. "Remember she is under Laird Dristan's protection. Do not harm her."

"Harm her? What jest is this, Kenna? I could no more harm the Lady Jade than I could my own sister."

Kenna peered at him overly long, making Thomas feel as though he had done some wrong. "Very well, Sir Thomas, but treat her with care. She has had a bit of a shock," she replied, afore turning her attention back to the lady upon the bed. "Jade, I know this is all new tae ye, but as Zoe has told ye, ye must think of this as a journey and the possibilities it may offer ye."

"Thank you, Kenna," Jade stated in a soft tone.

Thomas's stomach lurched in nervous jitters just to hear the sound of her voice.

Kenna nodded. "Please call out if ye have need of Lady Amiria or me. I will ensure a servant is just outside the door in the event ye need aid."

Thomas held open the door. Once Kenna left, he closed it and put the bolt in place to ensure their privacy. Jade quickly moved off the bed to stand behind a chair, clutching the wood with white knuckles, as if that would protect her. Her green eyes appeared damp and overly bright whilst she gasped and expelled her breath as though pained.

"I shall not harm you, my lady, but you and I must needs have speech," he stated carefully, afore nodding to the vacant seat. "May I?"

He observed her slow nod, and he went to sit afore the fire. Her expressions changed from fear to curiosity, and he hid the smile that threatened to form upon his lips.

"Your name is Thomas," she stated the obvious and finally took a seat opposite him, but she perched on the edge of her chair, at the ready to take flight if the need arose.

Thomas leaned back, attempting to appear calm

when he was anything but composed. "Aye, I am Thomas Kincaid, lately of Berwyck, and you are one of those future women who continues to plague this place."

"How do you know that?" she questioned, afore reaching for the jug of wine and pouring a cup. She offered him the chalice, and when their hands briefly touched, tingling sensations ran up his arm.

"We have met afore in my dreams. I will assume the same holds true for you since you knew my name as well."

"Yes... I have dreamed of you, too," she whispered, afore standing to pace the length of the room. "How is this even possible?"

Thomas shrugged, but he watched her every move, expecting her to disappear from view. "One does not tend to question such a gift, or so I have heard from the others who came afore you."

She cocked her head to one side as though reliving some memory. "A gift or a curse?" she whispered, afore she crossed her arms and placed her hands beneath her underarms as though hugging herself.

"I would prefer to think on it as a gift and certainly nary a curse that you are here with us."

"I am a long way from home, Thomas," she murmured, her eyes glistening with unshed tears.

"Perchance 'tis a Christmas blessing you appear to us for the holiday," he mused aloud. He leaned his arms upon the chair, his hands forming a steeple whilst inspecting her further. "Will you be missed? In your own time, that is?"

She shook her head, and Thomas was thoroughly captivated as her blonde hair swayed to and fro. "No. Well, that isn't necessarily true, I suppose. I have a few friends who might wonder where I am, but I have no family that I can claim."

He nodded, feeling her plight. "I, too, am without my family, although I had hoped such circumstances might change in my future. Berwyck has been my home now for many a year. The MacLaren clan took me in when my father disowned me."

Jade stopped her pacing. "Oh, Thomas, I'm so sorry. How horrible that must have been for you."

Thomas let out a low curse. "I am not certain why I even shared such a private matter with you, my lady."

"You don't have to call me that."

"Call you what?" he asked, pondering where he had erred.

"*My lady.* You don't have to call me that."

Thomas's mouth dropped open. Was she mayhap of yeoman stock or a woman of ill repute? He frowned for he had never thought of her as such when he dreamed of her. "Of course, I do. You are a lady, are you not?"

She laughed, and the pleasant sound rang through the room like a fresh breath of springtime. "Well, I *am* a woman, Thomas, but I certainly don't have a title or anything. I'm just *me*... Jade... from America."

A-mer-i-ca, he silently mouthed the words of her

origins. "You *are* a long way from home, for I have not heard of such a place."

"So, I have been told. Out of place and time it appears," she whispered so softly, he almost missed her words.

Silence descended upon the room with only the crackling fire to break the mood that had come upon them. He stood and went to her.

He was pleasantly surprised when she watched him as carefully as he observed her. "You are not afraid of me?"

A small smile lit her face. "No, of course not, unless you think I should be."

"Nay, I do not," he answered honestly before giving her a short bow. "Mayhap, we should start again. I am Sir Thomas, ever at your service, my lady."

"And I'm Jade. A pleasure to finally meet you, Sir Thomas." A short giggle escaped her afore she held out her hand for him to take.

"I am certain the pleasure is mine," he murmured. Bending to brush a kiss across her knuckles, his eyes widened when he became distracted by a strange glow coming from her opposite hand. 'Twas then that he recognized she wore his ring!

Suddenly, her left arm swept around his neck with alarming speed. The force brought their bodies together, and he could feel for himself when Jade attempted to catch her breath. "Thomas! I swear I didn't do that on purpose."

"Aye, I know," he muttered as his eyes widened in surprise when a power bigger than either of them could have imagined began to bring their lips closer together.

"Thomas..." she said in a breathy whisper.

"Jade..." he returned as their breaths mingled on a heartbeat afore they surrendered to their first real kiss.

CHAPTER 8

Jade was unsure what madness had overcome her to be kissing a man she barely knew, but, in many ways, she felt as though Thomas had always been a part of her. Crazy as it may seem to even have such thoughts, she gave in to the invisible energy surrounding and pulling them together.

The moment their lips touched, everything changed. Where before she felt as though she were being forced into something she didn't want, now, it was as if this was where she was always meant to be. With Thomas... in his arms... kissing him with all the love she could muster up for another human being.

Their kiss ended just as quickly as it had started. Their breaths ragged, they could only stare into each other eyes. Thomas reached down to caress her cheek, and a sense of wonderment filled her, knowing she had truly crossed time. He gave her a half smile as though he had heard her thoughts before he leaned down to taste what she now freely offered. It was as though they were now in control of their destiny.

Thomas deepened their kiss, and she heard his moan of pleasure even as she held back one of her own. It wasn't as if she hadn't been kissed before, but there was a reason she had remained single for so long and not married right out of high school like so many had done. No man had ever stepped into her life that seemed to be the other half of herself or just the piece of her that had been missing. She had sworn to herself she would never settle, but with Thomas, she had an instant connection she knew she would never find again in any other man. In an instant, the universe tilted as though they became as one, almost as though Zoe's words pulled them together from across the centuries.

As though she watched the scene in a movie theater, his arm wrapped around her waist, and he held her even tighter, bending her over. He made her swoon as no other man had ever done before. Her hand reached up and took ahold of his hair. Gosh, she never wanted to let him go. Emptiness surrounded her when he abruptly tore his lips from hers and pushed away from her. The cooler air of the room coming into contact with her flushed skin caused her to shiver.

He muttered something, possibly in Gaelic, giving Jade the impression he was of Scottish descent. But whatever his words meant, Jade couldn't understand any of them. He began to pace the room, much like she had done but moments before. She went to him and gently laid her hand upon his arm.

"What's the matter?" she asked, almost afraid to hear his answer.

He stared at her hand for several minutes until his words exploded from his lips. "*St. Michael's wings!* Where did you come by this?" he growled out before taking her hand and inspecting the ring she couldn't seem to get off her finger. He began to pull at the shiny gold band, but it wouldn't budge for him any more than it had moved for her.

Roughly, she tore her hand from his. "Stop that. You're hurting me," she shouted.

"I did not mean to cause you harm, but how came you by this ring?" he questioned again, his frown deepening.

Gazing down at the object of his concern, she held the ring close to her chest, hugging her hand as though it was wounded. If anything, the jewelry was her one way to return home, or so she guessed. She could not let him have it. Not at any cost, no matter the thoughts that had just gone through her head about the two of them belonging together.

His angry stance told her much, causing her thoughts to jumble around inside her head. She almost laughed out loud at the absurdity of her whole situation if it were to be believed. Time travel? *Please...* Yet how could she possibly wrap her head around the fact she appeared to be in some bedchamber in a medieval castle, let alone come to care for a complete stranger with just one kiss?

As far-fetched as all that was happening may have seemed, what was even more troubling was how hurt she felt now that Thomas was looking at her with nothing but suspicion. It was as if what they had just shared meant nothing to him, while ownership of the ring was his true obsession.

"I think you should leave," she warned, moving behind the chair to protect herself from him, or maybe, from herself for she had the sudden urge to jump into his arms.

"Jade, let me explain," he stated, moving toward her.

She halted his progress by holding up her hand. "I need time to think, Thomas. Please leave this room."

"You do not understand," he attempted again.

"I don't have to understand anything right now except the fact that I've asked you to leave."

He raked his hands through his dark hair, causing the ends to stand up in several places. His appearance was so adorable, just like from their dream, but she would not give in to the smile attempting to replace the stern expression she wished him to see.

"You will come down to the Great Hall for the evening meal, although the offerings will be meager 'til the morrow when we shall feast in celebration of our Savior's birth."

"Are you ordering or asking me to come down to join you?" Jade held her breath, waiting for his answer. If he planned to boss her about, then she knew there would be no chance for them. She wouldn't bow down to any man, neither here in the past or in her future life.

His gaze leveled upon her body, and her cheeks flushed again when she witnessed the desire reflected in his eyes. He gave a short bow. "'Tis a request, my lady."

She nodded, knowing he had chosen wisely. "Then I shall see you later, although I have no idea what is beyond these four walls."

"I shall send a servant to find you *suitable* attire, along with ensuring you find your way to the hall at the appointed hour," he stated as he took in her modern-day clothing.

Jade whispered a soft *thank you* before he left, closing the door quietly behind him. Running across the room, her fingers took hold of the bolt upon the door, sliding the metal into place. Taking huge gulps of air to calm her nerves, she turned to lean her back against the door until her breathing returned to normal.

She was safe, at least for the time being. Pushing off the door, Jade returned to the fire and took up the chalice she had offered Thomas. Taking a sip and hoping the wine would calm her nerves, she began to stare into the flames, wondering what in the hell she had gotten herself into, or better yet, when in the world would she would ever wake up from this crazy-ass dream.

Thomas entered the Great Hall, filled with the knights who quietly ate from platters of fish upon the long tables. 'Twas relatively silent, given the Advent season, and Thomas was looking forward to something on his trencher besides bread or fish. After the morrow's morning Mass, those who dwelled at Berwyck would finally have their bellies full.

The wine, if that was what this could be called, had been watered down 'til it had no flavor, and Thomas barely touched his chalice nor the food set afore him. Nay. He was too anxious to eat whilst he awaited the appearance of his lady.

He had been a fool earlier, and he must needs ask forgiveness from Lady Jade both for kissing her and his hostile behavior. Their kiss had sent Thomas into a whirlwind of thoughts and awoke parts of him that had been dormant for far longer than he cared to admit even to himself. His anger afterward had been appalling and he was more upset with himself than with the lady. But how was he to explain the sudden urge to thoroughly kiss the woman when a force beyond his ken threw them together?

Thomas had left her chamber feeling the fool, especially when he had made an attempt to remove his family ring from her finger without success. Going to his own room, he changed into fresh garments afore finally making his way down the turret stairs. As he made his way to the raised dais with the lord and lady of the keep, he heard murmurs of discontent from the knights who were only at Berwyck for training. His normal place was to sit with the rest of the personal guardsmen. Sitting next to Lady Amiria made him feel out of place and as though he was being inspected by the entire company of knights. Thomas could only think 'twas a place of honor to be sitting next to Lady Amiria, and he assumed 'twas because of the vision who now came into view.

Jade's blonde tresses had been pulled up from her shoulders. A small, thin veil adorned her head and trailed down her back. The sleeves of the white under tunic came down to a point upon her wrists. The green kirtle she had donned was only surpassed by the brilliant color of her eyes.

He was about to rise and go to her 'til another figure rushed to her side, giving her a formal bow. Thomas's teeth clenched as he watched Gaillard all but trifle with his lady's confusion as she took in the hall. He had a certain amount of satisfaction whilst she ignored the knight afore her, and her gaze searched the room until their eyes locked. Her smile lit up her entire visage, and Thomas became lost, especially when his heart began to beat furiously within his chest.

God's Bones, what is happening to us?

CHAPTER 9

Jade's breath hitched as she saw Thomas from across the room. Had it only been a couple of hours since she had been with him? She offered him a smile and was pleased when he returned her gesture. Unfortunately, the knight who was grasping for her attention interrupted their moment.

She listened with half an ear as he rambled on about his knighthood, family, wealth, and his estate. He continued to brag on about the number of coins in his coffers until Jade frowned in displeasure. *Damn, he's full of himself,* she thought even while an instant dislike for the fellow came over her.

"You must be famished after your ordeal, my lady," the knight proclaimed with what appeared to be smug insincerity. "Having been thrown from your horse leaving you hurt and unconscious in the snow would certainly require the aid of Berwyck's healer to see you on the mend."

"My horse?" she questioned, wondering how on earth this guy thought she actually knew how to ride such an animal. *I wasn't thrown from my horse, you idiot, I fell through time*, she thought, knowing she couldn't voice such a statement.

"Aye, your horse," he replied with a quizzical look. "'Tis the account I heard tell from Lord Dristan on why I found you in such a condition."

So, that's what they told everyone instead of the truth of my being from the future because really... who would believe such an outrageous story? God forbid what would happen to her if these people knew where she really came from. A brief image of being burned at the stake caused her to gulp hard.

"Ah, yes, my horse, the unruly beast," she finally replied, watching his smile broaden across his face again. She'd seen his type a million times before and usually stayed clear of handsome men who thought they were God's gift to women.

Her eyes automatically sought out Thomas, and the man before her must have seen who she was focusing her attention on. Gaillard's frown was fierce when he took her elbow to lead her into the room. "You must forget all about Sir Thomas and his ghastly attempts to win your affections."

What the hell? Jade yanked her arm away from him even while the knight began to give her a frightening scowl. "What did you say your name was?" she asked, trying to divert his attention from taking her anywhere.

"Did you not take heed of my earlier words, dear lady? I am Gaillard de Rowen, and as soon as I may gain permission from Lord Dristan, you shall be my wife."

An unladylike laugh escaped her. "Yeah... sorry, buddy, but that's not happening."

She left him sputtering behind her as she quickly lifted the hem of her dress and moved forward into the hall. Her only thought was to get to Thomas. She had only made it half way across the room before he met her and bowed.

"Did he harm you?"

"No, of course not, but Gaillard does have some ridiculous idea in his head that he and I should be married. He plans to talk to Lord Dristan about it."

"I shall kill him with my bare hands for making such an assumption," Thomas hissed, taking a menacing step forward.

"Don't waste any energy on him, Thomas."

Jade laced her arm through his, and the tension in his arm lessened before he took ahold of her hand. He raised it to his lips, and she could have sighed at such a romantic gesture. No one did this anymore in modern times, and she was sorry to see such a custom lost when it was so touching.

"If you insist," he murmured, while his blue-gray eyes leveled on her waiting for her response.

"Yes, I do. He's not worth it," she replied, "and there

are far more important things I can think of to discuss than that arrogant knight."

"Then come and let us eat. 'Tis a meager meal, but I promise on the morrow, we shall feast. Lord Dristan and Lady Amiria will ensure all are well taken care of after fasting for so long." He began escorting her past several tables of knights, who stopped eating just to stare when she walked by.

"And will *you* also make sure I am taken care of?" Her eyes widened at what her words could possibly mean to the medieval man who halted in his steps.

A roguish grin plastered itself across his features. He was certainly pleased with her words, and he appeared even more attractive as his eyes seemed to twinkle in delight.

He held her gaze before he lifted a finger to slowly caress her cheek. "Most assuredly, *mo ghràdh*."

His slip of what she assumed was a Scottish endearment made her shiver and she wondered why he didn't use such a sexy enunciation all the time instead of sounding English. She had always been a sucker for a man with an accent, and even she could understand the implication. She reached up to move her fingers along the edge of his shirt, *tunic* she mentally corrected herself, and was impressed he had taken time to change his clothes from earlier.

"You look very handsome tonight, good sir," she murmured, almost easily falling into the role she was currently required to play.

"And I have never seen a more beautiful woman," he replied, and she could see that he spoke from the heart.

"Thomas!" a voice called out.

Thomas did not take his eyes from her but instead, called back over his shoulder, "Aye, my lord?"

"Do you plan to stand there all eve with the Lady Jade, or will you see her to our table so she may eat her fill? The poor woman must be famished given how long it must have been since she has last eaten," Dristan bellowed, causing several knights to burst out in laughter.

"Coming, my lord," Thomas answered before tucking her hand again in the crook of his arm. "Shall we, Lady Jade?"

Her mouth went suddenly dry, and she couldn't seem to form any words so instead, she just nodded. Thomas escorted her through the rest of the hall until they stood before the lord and lady of Berwyck. Thomas bowed and not knowing what else to do, Jade bobbed a short curtsey.

Lord Dristan stood. "Lady Jade, you are a most welcome guest, and I offer you my protection whilst you are here," he said, before turning to the knight to his right. "Bertram, move next to Lady Amiria so I may converse with Lady Jade, who has traveled far to be with us today."

Thomas leaned down to whisper in her ear that Bertram was the captain of Lord Dristan's personal guardsmen. They moved around the long table, and once she was seated, Jade felt dwarfed sitting between the two massive men. Thomas filled a trencher before nudging it closer to her, giving her the impression they were to share the food. Her eyes darted around her immediate surroundings. *Did it suddenly get overly hot in here?* Sweat beaded on her upper lip, while her pulse began to race. *Good lord...* She really was back in the twelfth century and in an English castle of all places. What the hell was she supposed to do now?

Thomas noticed Jade's moment of panic when her face went ashen. Reaching down beneath the table, he took ahold of her hand and gave her shaking limb a reassuring squeeze. She gripped his hand hard enough to break a bone if she continued.

"Easy now, my lady. No harm shall befall you whilst you are in my care," he murmured, attempting to set her fears to rest.

She turned in his direction, her green eyes filling with unshed tears. "Please don't leave me, Thomas," she croaked out. "You are the only person who I feel connected to in this place."

Her hushed tone went straight to his heart, and he pulled her hand to hold it over his chest.

"Never," he vowed. "*Time* has brought us together. I would be a fool to let a lady such as you slip through my grasp."

"You don't even know me. How can you make such a promise?"

"I know *you* just as you know *me*. If we search our hearts, we shall find all our answers. There is nothing we cannot conquer as long as we are together."

Her smile was hesitant, and he reached over to wipe away the single tear escaping down her cheek.

"That's a pretty big statement considering we've only just met."

"Sometimes it takes a miracle to find your heart's desire," he replied honestly, "or even an instant in time."

"You seem pretty sure we're meant to be a couple. Exactly how much wine have you been drinking?" she teased before looking into his chalice.

"Upon my honor, I am not so far gone into my cups, my lady," Thomas sputtered.

"Are you sure?" Her brow lifted as she inspected him. "You're not going all white-girl wasted on me, are you?"

His frown creased his forehead for he was at a loss to the meaning of her words. Future women and their ways of speech would make any medieval man slightly crazed. How did Riorden and Fletcher ever survive?

"I am not even sure how I can or should respond to such speech," he groaned out at last. "What the devil is this white-girl wasted?"

A laugh escaped her. "If you ever happen to see me totally drunk and spewing out my emotions in a hot mess, you'll understand the meaning."

He shook his head, not daring to ask about her *hot mess* comment. "I assure you, Lady Jade, I am not one to go about getting drunk and then letting my mouth run amuck."

Her face turned to a pinkish hue. "I'm sorry for teasing you, Thomas. This medieval life might take some getting used to. Do you forgive me?"

"Of course," he said, still confused as to how their discussion had made such a turn.

"Then let's go back to the serious part of our lovely conversation before I made light of your beautiful words. It was all very romantic, by the way."

"Are you perchance jesting with me?" he asked, for he was generally not one to bare his soul so openly to another. He did not wish her to think him weak.

"No, not now. Your earlier words were what any woman would long to hear from someone they care about."

"You care for me then?"

"I'm sure that's why I'm here in this place and time. You spoke of your heart's desire and finding it in just an instant. Did you learn all this from the one kiss we shared?"

"I would spend all of my days searching for you if I must, just to receive one last kiss from your lips, Jade," Thomas replied, realizing he meant every word he had spoken.

His earlier thoughts of binding her to him all because of the ring no longer had the same meaning.

They were connected in a way far bigger than just the two of them.

Her mouth dropped open in startled surprise afore she recovered from his words. She leaned forward and reached out to cup his cheek. "I believe you," she said with all honesty, at least as far as Thomas could tell. "Funny how just yesterday you were nothing but a dream, and today, here I am sitting next to you. You *are* real, aren't you?"

He chuckled when she lightly poked him in the chest. "Only you can answer such a question, my lady," he replied in a husky tone.

Before he changed his mind, Thomas quickly leaned down to offer a soft kiss upon her lips. A sigh of contentment left her mouth, but afore he could respond, he heard a low warning groan coming from his liege lord.

Lord Dristan placed his arm upon the table close to his lady's side of the trencher. "By *God's bone's*, Thomas, you shall remain a respectable distance from this woman or face me on the lists," he cautioned warily. "You certainly should not be kissing her in my hall and in front of the entire garrison!"

"Understood, my liege," Thomas answered, afore sitting back into his chair. "I best behave myself. No sense getting on the wrong side of the Devil's Dragon," he told her with a wink.

Her eyes widened. "Did I just hear you call him the Devil's Dragon?"

'Twas Thomas's turn to laugh even whilst Dristan mockingly grunted some off-handed reply and returned to his meal. "Aye, but I shall leave the telling of his story for another time."

"I'm not sure I want to hear it, let alone know why he's called such a frightening name."

Lady Amiria laughed whilst apparently listening in on their conversation. "Do not let his reputation fool you, Jade. My Dristan has a fiery roar, but he is hardly the Devil some take him for."

Dristan choked on his wine afore turning his gaze to his wife. "You do me a disservice, madam. How do you expect the men to respect me if you make me out to be less than a fearsome lord?"

Amiria reached over to pat his hand in what appeared as a gesture to soothe his rising temper. "The men respect you, my lord, without your mighty reputation," she said, afore looking around her husband to stare at Jade. "You have nothing to fear from him. Besides, our story has one of those... what did Lady Katherine call them?" she asked Dristan.

"Happily ever after, endings," he growled out, "or some such lovesick nonsense."

Amiria gave him a none too gentle swat afore scowling at him. "Aye, *happily* ever after lest he does not behave himself and I take him to task for being overbearing."

The couple returned to a private conversation between themselves, giving Thomas leave to return his attention to the lady at his side. "The food grows cold. Let us eat, then enjoy what we can of the remainder of the eve."

He took her hand again to place a kiss upon her fingertips afore returning to dine from their trencher. They conversed throughout the meal as though they were long-lost friends. Her sweet laughter rang out, and he could not remember an occasion when he had last felt so content. The more they spoke, the more interested he became in learning all there was to know of this mysterious lady who had crossed time for him.

The night passed all too quickly as far as Thomas was concerned, and afore long, Lord Dristan and Lady Amiria were escorting Jade from the hall. He watched when she turned one last time to wave at him afore she disappeared up the turret stairs.

He frowned, not because of her inevitable departure, but because he was not the only man who watched her leave. Nay, he was not pleased when he noticed Gaillard observing her with lust-filled eyes. Thomas's fists clenched at his side knowing the knight needed watching, especially where the lovely Lady Jade was concerned.

CHAPTER 10

Jade listened to those assembled in the chapel. They all voiced a reverent *amen*. Earlier, she shouldn't have been surprised when she was ushered to sit in the row of benches reserved for the lord and lady of Berwyck's family. She could only be made to feel that she was in a place of honor. Yet all this gallantry and *my lady* business took some getting used to. At least she had seen enough movies or read enough romance novels to understand the fundamentals of twelfth-century living. *But will it be enough to pass among them for any length of time?* Maybe, the questions she should ask herself were how in the world was she going to get herself home, or did she wish to stay?

She had been thankful when Thomas had been allowed to sit next to her, and he seemed happy to also have her near. It wasn't as though she had never been in a church before. No, that wasn't the problem. The problem was she couldn't understand a word the priest was saying. The entire Mass had been said in Latin. She tried not to think about the fact that this was a daily ritual with the people of this time. She was unsure how she would survive what she would consider an ordeal.

Sitting on the bench or kneeling on the cold stone floor for what seemed like hours had taken a toll on her body, and Jade was slow to rise. Her knees wobbled, and Thomas was quick to rush to her aid. His arm snaked securely around her waist, leaving Jade no choice but to take hold of his tunic for additional support.

Green eyes met blue-gray as air rushed into her lungs when she came into contact with his extremely muscular chest. The sound of someone clearing his throat had them turning their attention to the priest. Father Donovan wasn't pleased, and they quickly drew apart with a hasty apology.

Thomas began escorting Jade from the chapel but turned to pull up the hood of her cloak before opening the door. The air was crisp as a blast of wind snapped at her face. The newly fallen snow sparkled like diamonds but was also blinding, causing Jade to shield her eyes. She stood amazed at the view. The castle keep towered at least four stories high, and she could hear the sound of the ocean in the distance. She really *had* traveled through time because there was no way this was San Francisco!

"This is a lot to take in," she said quietly to Thomas,

who took her about the waist and gently guided her over an icy patch on the ground.

"You are handling this whole experience well, Jade," he replied. "You do not mind that I call you by your given name, do you?"

She gave a short laugh. "Actually, I prefer it. It's certainly way more personal than all this *my lady* stuff, although a woman could get used to that if she's not careful."

Entering the keep, the delicious aroma of roasted meat caused Jade's mouth to water. Apparently, she was hungrier than she thought. Watching in fascination, her eyes traveled to the numerous servants who scurried about with platters filled to capacity as the occupants of the hall began to enter. Once she was seated, she stared in wonder at the bounty before her, while Thomas heaped food onto their trencher until it almost overflowed.

"You must be *really* hungry," she teased him.

"You are not?" he asked before he dismissed a servant and took over the task of pouring wine into her chalice.

"Well, I am, but there's enough food here for several meals. I'm not used to eating so much meat."

"We have been fasting for nigh unto a month."

Advent, she thought, remembering Thomas's earlier words. Before she could answer him, the sound of trumpets blared into the room. A huge platter was carried in with much ceremony.

Her eyes widened. "Is that a pig's head?"

"Boar. 'Tis very good. You must needs try it."

She gulped, looking at the charred thing set before Lord Dristan and his lady who appeared pleased with the offering before them. "I think, I'll pass."

He shrugged. "As you wish, but you must eat your fill. I will not have a lady in my care wasting away because she forgot to break her fast," he said, pointing to the food before them as he began eating with the gusto of a starving man.

She picked at the food, finding most of the meat quite tasty. The vegetables were too overcooked for her liking, and she would have preferred a nice salad. Since that wasn't an option set before her, she continued to nibble at the food until she was full. Still, Thomas consumed most of what was left on the trencher. Jade sipped her wine, finding it far more intoxicating than what she had previously tasted, or perhaps, it was the man next to her that made her feel lightheaded.

She watched the room in curiosity. Christmas was far more understated than what she was used to as she attempted to remind herself where she really was. There was no tree with bulbs or tinsel with presents underneath, waiting to be unwrapped or any other decorations she expected from modern times. No bright twinkling lights, no red poinsettias, just an everyday hall in the twelfth century without any form of commercialism. *This is actually kind of refreshing*, Jade thought when she realized how the true meaning of the holiday tended to get lost in her world.

"Is something wrong?" Thomas leaned over.

Her heart flipped at the heavenly scent coming from this gorgeous medieval knight. The hint of warm spices seemed to surround him, giving Jade goosebumps, and she did everything in her power not to put her face into his hair just so she could smell him to her heart's content. Good Lord, what was this man unintentionally doing to her?

She took a deep breath in a shallow attempt to calm her nerves that became scattered in a good way whenever she was near Thomas.

"No, nothing is wrong. In fact, everything is so *right,* it scares me," she stated.

One corner of his mouth turned up, and his eyes sparkled in delight. "Then you are pleased to be here," he said, waiting for her answer before taking a sip from his chalice.

Pleased, yes. Scared out of my wits? Yes. Wanting to return home? Possibly, Jade pondered in confusion. But really, what was there for her to return to back in Michigan? A couple of friends but no one who would truly miss her. Certainly, there wasn't any family waiting for her with open arms since she had been lost in the foster care system until she became an adult and had been forced to make her own way in the world.

"Jade—"

She shook her head from the memories she'd rather

leave buried in the past and returned her attention to the knight who now gazed upon her with worried eyes. "Sorry. What were you saying?"

"'Tis not of import," Thomas replied, attempting to relax in his chair, but he was failing miserably.

A slight frown marred his features, and Jade had the sudden urge to see him smile instead. Just as swiftly as that thought popped into her head, another one entered her mind. He had spent far too many years burdened with the actions of his youth. The image of a young Thomas flinging the same ring now stuck on her finger off into the woods replayed inside her head. She wondered if what she thought was a mere hallucination from jet lag was actually true.

She placed her hand upon his arm, and her thumb rubbed the fabric of his tunic in a soothing motion.

"I think whatever you have on your mind is very important. Please tell me what you're thinking," she urged in a soft plea to hear the thoughts of this medieval man. She could almost hear the musings going on inside his head. *He's just as confused as I am with everything that is happening between us at such an alarming speed.*

He took a deep breath and then another sip of his wine before placing the goblet back down upon the table. "I was asking if you are pleased to be here."

In that moment, Jade knew she wanted to see where all this could go between them or even if it were possible for her to stay here in the past.

She took up his chalice and placed her lips to the

spot where his mouth had just touched it. His eyes widened before a grin split his face.

She returned his smile. "Yes, Thomas. I believe I am..." Her words trailed off to be lost with the sounds of the busy hall.

If she had looked down upon her hand, she would have seen the ring giving off a low, golden glow.

Let their journey begin.

CHAPTER 11

Thomas led his stallion toward the stable even though his mind wandered to the incredible woman who walked across the inner bailey with Lady Amiria. His body could still feel the warmth of Jade's whilst she had ridden behind him across the strand.

'Twas hard to believe only a fortnight ago, Jade had been but a dream to him, an imaginary figure haunting his mind since he had been but a lad of ten and four summers. Now, he had a difficult time coming to terms with her possibly returning back to her life in the future. He had been enjoying her company so much of late that he did not wish to see her leave. Ever. He gave a hefty sigh.

The weather had become unusually warm causing much of the snow to melt away. If Thomas had not known what time of the year it was, he would have sworn spring was in the air. Because of their good fortune, Lord Dristan had thought an afternoon excursion would be a nice diversion, and anything would have been better than spending time on the lists. Thomas had been pleased to see Jade and Lady Amiria were to join them, along with Kenna and her husband Geoffrey.

"He is thunderstruck, my lord." Geoffrey chuckled, whilst assisting his lady down from her saddle. He then led his horse past Thomas. "Best get him inside with a mug of ale, or else he will be following your ward to declare his undying love."

Thomas muttered beneath his breath. He cared not to be the jest of any conversation, let alone to be ridiculed by those he trained with on a daily basis.

"Let the matter rest, Geoffrey, lest you wish to continue this conversation in the lists," he warned, whilst peering at the offensive knight.

Dristan pulled upon Thor's reins to halt his mighty steed. "Another of my knights lost to the arms of a good woman," he muttered. "Will I have anyone left to help defend my castle if this continues?"

Kenna pulled her cloak closer around her. "Ye should be ashamed tae be teasing Thomas," she said, wagging her finger at them. "We will have speech, Thomas. I believe there are many questions I may be able tae answer for ye."

Dristan called out to a lad who came and took Thomas's horse. "Off you go then, Thomas. Heed

Kenna's words, for she is generally helpful to those who find themselves with one of those future ladies."

Thomas watched his horse being led away afore extending his arm to Kenna. They made their way to the inner bailey and her hut. When he opened the door for Berwyck's healer to enter, he inhaled the scent of herbs hanging on ropes from the ceiling. She crossed the room to stoke her fire and then collected various herbs that she crushed in a nearby pestle. She swung a metal pot over the fire and placed the herbs within, causing the room to fill with a pleasant fragrance.

"Sit," she ordered and waited for him to take the chair next to her. "Ask me what ye wish tae know, and I will tell ye what I see."

"I do not know where to begin," he replied, casually looking around the small dwelling.

"At the beginning, of course. 'Tis where every tale begins, is this not so?" She took a ladle and scooped some of her concoction into a mug afore handing it to him. "Take a drink first afore ye start, but ye can forget about what happened with yer family afore ye came tae Berwyck."

"You saw what happened? How I lost the relic of my ancestors?"

Kenna peered at him with her odd green eyes afore she placed her own mug down on a table. "'Tis not yer fault ye lost the ring, Thomas."

He choked on his drink and began to cough. "Surely

you jest, Kenna. I tossed the damn thing into the forest when I thought it was witchery that I saw Jade in her future world."

She went about tsk-tsking afore patting his hand. "If ye had not tossed it, the ring would have disappeared anyway. Ye were not ready for its gift."

"What gift? The ring was the reason my own father disowned me in the first place, forever keeping me from my family and birthright. 'Tis no gift!" he fumed, raking his hand through his hair with trembling fingers whilst he attempted to listen to what the woman afore him had to say.

"The ring's gift isna that yer father lost his faith in ye."

"Then what the hell is going on, and why does Jade have it?"

Kenna's finger lingered upon her lips as though she debated on whether or not she should tell him the secret the ring held. "The true gift of the ring is tae bring those together who search for love."

"'Tis impossible," he huffed, even whilst a vague memory of his father's voice whispered across his mind.

"Is it? Then how is it ye saw Jade when ye were but a lad and then also in yer dreams once ye were a man full-grown? Time may have kept ye apart, but the ring is what brought ye together."

Thomas pondered her words with a frown. "She crossed time like those who came to Berwyck afore her.

That is how she came to be here," he stated, with a confidence he did not necessarily feel.

"Nay, she did not. 'Twas the ring, Thomas. Those who are truly worthy will find their true love, and once found, the ring shall disappear 'til its magic is needed yet again. There were those who found the ring over the centuries after ye lost it in yer youth. Some but touched it for a moment afore 'twas lost or disappeared. Others found a love worth risking everything they held dear just so they can be together. There will also be those who will find it yet again beyond what even *I* can see."

He scowled, thinking of how ridiculous this whole situation had become. Far-fetched for certain but yet how else could he explain Jade's ownership of his family's ring?

"When I first saw the ring upon Jade's finger, I tried to take it from her. It would not come off no matter how hard I pulled. Yet I have seen her twirling the loose band upon her finger. I do not understand why even she cannot seem to be rid of it."

"Ye canna take what is not freely given, Thomas. Ye both must choose yer heart's desire. Find love with each other or let Jade return tae her own place in time. 'Tis a decision ye both must willingly make and accept if ye wish tae be together, else ye risk tae lose far more than just the ring tae time."

"You have given me much to ponder, Kenna. Mayhap, Jade will just stay here whether she possesses the ring or not," he mused out loud. *Who is to say whether she stays here or returns?* He kept this notion to himself.

Kenna swatted at his arm as though she heard his inner thoughts. "Ye are not listening tae me, ye daft man. Do ye care for Jade, or do ye only wish tae own the ring?"

Thomas stood and paced the confines of the healer's small hut. "Of course, I care for the lady. We have spoken on many things and find we have a common accord, but we have never touched on the subject of the ring."

"If ye care for her, then ye must tell her afore 'tis too late. Only once ye both profess yer love can ye have everything ye have wanted these many years, Thomas."

His eyes widened. "You mean I could return home? I could take Jade with me and return to Lennox Castle with my honor restored?" he repeated, dumbstruck that he had not thought of this himself.

"If she gives ye the ring freely, anything is possible," Kenna replied with a soft smile.

"My thanks, Kenna, for your words of wisdom," Thomas said, afore he nodded and left the hut.

He began to cross the inner bailey, completely lost in thought, pondering how he would broach the subject of his feelings to a lady he had only known but a fortnight. Could love possibly find them in such a short amount of time? His words to Jade echoed in his mind, of finding his heart's desire in but an instant.

Thomas knew his answer, and his smile broadened

as he went to search for his beautiful lady, but nothing prepared him for the scream echoing from one of the upper floors of the keep. Terrified Jade was in need of his aid, he began to run as though their lives depended on him finding her.

CHAPTER 12

Jade swung the iron poker in front of her, brandishing it like a weapon. She was an idiot for sliding the bolt open to allow the person knocking free entrance to her room before asking who was on the other side. She had thought it was Thomas or Amiria and had nothing to worry about. Even back in her own time, she would have looked through the peephole before letting anyone enter. She was such an idiot, and now look what her carelessness had gotten her!

The sight of the long metal blade as his sword was released from the scabbard at the knight's side made Jade cringe in fear, not that she allowed such an emotion to cross her face. She refused to give this jerk the satisfaction of seeing she was scared. Her eyes darted back and forth as she watched the blade until it struck the iron from her now-numb fingers.

"Did you really think you could escape me so easily?" he taunted, coming toward her in a determined stride.

She began tossing items near her reach, anything to stop him from getting closer to her. A candlestick holder, a chalice, the pitcher of wine that shattered on the wall behind him when the damn villain ducked. Her supply was running out as she looked about for something else to throw at his head. His laughter rang out, and Jade realized her feeble attempts to thwart whatever objective he had in mind were of no use.

The only place she could run to escape him was the door. He knew her thoughts the moment they crossed her mind even though she still dodged around him in an effort to gain her freedom. He grabbed ahold of her hair, giving it a mighty yank and forcing a scream from her lips.

The sound echoed in the room, and Jade hoped that others would be able to hear her through the protective stones of her chamber.

"Let me go, Gaillard," she yelled, only to find herself being hurled face first against the door with a loud thump that left her dazed.

Gaillard wasted no time pushing her aside to take hold of the door latch. With her knees threatening to buckle beneath her wavering feet, he grabbed ahold of her waist in a tight squeeze. The sound of the door slamming into the wall when it opened ricocheted in her head as he dragged her down the passageway.

"I would have wed you to secure your fortune, but you left me with no choice."

"What fortune?" she hissed, while clawing at his arm. It was encased in chain mail and did little harm to him.

He gave an amused chuckle. "You cannot tell me, fair lady, that you have no monies to fill my coffers if you are the ward of the Devil's Dragon. Since he would not give his permission to wed, I shall demand a ransom for your return instead."

"Where the hell are you taking me? You can't just take someone against her will," she bellowed, while furiously thinking of some way to get away from this madman.

"'Tis not of import where I take you but more so that Dristan of Berwyck pays to keep you in the same condition as when you left." He laughed, coming to stand in front of a solid wall of stone. "Now where is it?" he said more or less to himself as his fingers began searching the rocks.

Jade heard a soft click, and the whole wall of stones swung inward on well-oiled hinges. She would have been impressed with the engineering, especially for medieval times, if it weren't for the fact this crazy ass person was grabbing a torch with one hand and pulling her into a darkened passageway with the other.

"Thomas," she screamed, even as the hidden doorway closed promptly behind her, cutting off her voice.

Her imagination ran wild as they began their descent down a rough stone stairway. Her fear of the black gloom surrounding them almost had her paralyzed and worried the torch would go out. They would be plunged into complete darkness, much like a coffin, and Jade wondered if following Gaillard for now might be in her best interest until she could think of another way to escape. No one would be able to locate her if the narrow walls caved in on her.

The cavern smelled of musty, wet dirt, reminding Jade of a basement after it had flooded. Still, they continued downward until she thought they had traversed the entire cliff Berwyck sat upon, which was probably not far from the truth. She began to hear the distant sound of the ocean's roar. Trembling, she could only wonder how Thomas would ever find her if Gaillard reached the beach, allowing him to escape.

She whispered a heartfelt prayer, knowing Thomas was her only hope of survival. Galliard was unrelenting in his pace, all the while grumbling about the injustice of his life. Jade remained silent, not wishing to further irritate the man. Still, the path spiraled downward. As his pace quickened at an alarming speed, she was thankful she was able to remain on her feet while her attacker all but dragged her into what she prayed wouldn't be her grave.

CHAPTER 13

Thomas had just reached the door to the keep when he heard his name being torn from Jade's lips from somewhere up above. His eyes traveled upward at the towering fortress. He reached for the latch 'til Kenna's voice came yelling at him from behind.

"Thomas," she called. "Get tae yer horse!"

"I must needs find Jade and go to her aid," he retorted, opening the door.

"Nay! Get tae yer horse, ye fool, afore 'tis tae late," she warned him whilst Dristan came upon them with his sword drawn. "My laird, ye must needs take Thomas tae the entrance of the hidden passageway upon the beach."

Dristan sputtered a curse. "Lady Jade knows nothing of such an escape route—"

Kenna's eyes were filled with worry when she finished his sentence. "—but Gaillard does."

"Bloody hell," Thomas replied, whilst his mind thought of what he would do to Gaillard if he but harmed one hair on Jade's head.

Dristan pulled at Thomas's arm. "Let us make haste!"

Thomas raced closely behind as they ran back toward the stables. Luckily, the stable lads had not yet had time to unsaddle their steeds, except for Geoffrey's. Grabbing the reins of their horses, they vaulted into their saddles whilst Dristan called out for others to follow. Geoffrey did not bother with a saddle but instead, swung up onto his horse and kicked the animal into motion.

The three knights galloped out of the barbican gateway. Onward they went, over the drawbridge, through the field separating the castle from the village, and down into the woods afore making their way onto the beach.

Clumps of sand and remaining snow flew behind Thomas whilst he drove his horse on to reach Jade. Memories assaulted his mind of times Amiria used the hidden passageway reserved for Berwyck's family to make her way to the beach. Her mother had told Thomas of such an escape route, and he had been honored she considered him such a part of her family that she would entrust him with its location. He had not thought anyone outside of the MacLaren's or Dristan's personal guardsmen knew of what he thought was a well-kept secret.

His heart leapt into his throat when his gaze went to the cliff, and he saw Gaillard and Jade appear through the foliage which kept the entrance hidden from view. Jade began screaming, and she made an attempt to dig her feet in the sand, but she was no match for the stronger knight, who continued to pull her toward his waiting horse.

The sound of their horses' thundering hooves drew Gaillard's attention to the rescue party as they neared. He gave Jade a mighty shove and drew his sword, even whilst Thomas leapt from his horse to advance.

"You worthless cur! I will gladly see to your early demise for daring to take that which I hold dear!" Thomas declared, pulling out his own blade.

Gaillard spat upon the ground. "Not if I kill you first!"

The two men began to circle around one another even whilst Dristan and Geoffrey dismounted and went to Jade's side. Dristan helped her to her feet, and the trio moved a distance away, giving Thomas free rein to dispatch the knight afore him.

Swords clashed over and over again, and still, Thomas gave no quarter. He had not trained with the Devil's Dragon all these years to easily lose at hand-to-hand combat, especially with someone who but recently joined the garrison. Nay, he would fight to the death if need be to keep Jade safe. Thomas thrust forward again and smirked in triumph when Gaillard's sword flew from his hand

But Thomas was not done with him yet. Nay! He stepped forward and the bones of Gaillard's nose crunched beneath Thomas's fist. He continued his assault until the knight fell to his knees. Yanking at the Gaillard's surcoat, Thomas raised his fist to finish him off, but the downward plunge was halted when he heard Jade calling out his name.

"Thomas," she yelled with tears running down her cheeks. "Please do not kill him because of me! He's not worth it."

There could be no mistaking this woman's tender heart, and she would have much to learn if she were to stay in this time.

"You are lucky my lady is merciful and spares your life," he sneered. "I would have liked nothing better than to send you back to hell where you belong."

He gave Gaillard a mighty shove, watched the knight fall backward into the sand, and then made his way towards his lady.

Jade detached herself from Dristan and ran into his open arms. He brushed the tears from her face afore leaning down and placing his forehead upon her own.

"You gave me such a fright, my lady," he murmured, feeling her arms wind around his waist. "I swear I plan to never let you out of my sight again."

Her green eyes sparkled with happiness. "Promises, promises. Why don't you just kiss me to seal our fate?"

He gave a hearty laugh afore he leaned down to

thoroughly kiss his lovely lady, hoping they would have a lifetime of kisses to share.

CHAPTER 14

Jade sat in her bedchamber, twirling the ring upon her finger and staring off into the fire. The day's earlier events had left her out of sorts. Thomas's kiss filled her heart with joy, but being kidnapped, then watching Gaillard being led off by Dristan's men to reside in some pit in the depths of Berwyck's bowels, would leave anyone shaking in their boots.

She had come to a decision tonight, and she hoped she wouldn't be making a mistake. She could only guess at the late hour of the night, but she had a hunch if she called for him, Thomas would come to her chamber. She looked at the ring as it gave off a soft glow.

She smiled while twirling the gold around her finger once more, the guiding star appearing even more pronounced as though it had led her to the man from her dreams.

"Come to me, Thomas," she whispered softly into the night.

She stood and poured them a chalice of wine, confident he would be shortly knocking on her door.

Even though she was prepared for the sound, her heart still leapt into her throat at the soft rap. She went to the portal but hesitated before sliding the bolt open. She had already learned that lesson and would not make the same mistake twice.

"Who is it?" she asked, leaning in to the wood to hear the response.

"Thomas," he answered, before she slid the bolt and opened the door.

He stood there, her handsome medieval knight who made her heart soar. She smiled at the knowledge that if the ring had brought them together, their love needed no magic to last forever.

She opened the door wider. "Come in," she urged, waving her hand inside.

He waited in the passageway in indecision, a frown marring his features while he took in her nightclothes. "I cannot. 'Tis not proper, and Lord Dristan would have my head on a pike outside his gates if I would dishonor your reputation."

She resisted the urge to giggle, knowing he was completely serious. She took his hand and pulled him inside. He flinched when she shut the door behind him.

"I'm a modern woman, Thomas. I know there is no

dishonor with you coming inside my room, just as I know I'm perfectly safe here with you."

Thomas muttered something beneath his breath, pointing toward the night-rail she wore. "You tempt me beyond what a mere mortal man can endure, *mo ghràdh*, but I could not deny myself the opportunity to learn if what I heard was true."

"Did you hear something?" she asked with a small laugh, already knowing his answer.

"I heard you call to me, or did I imagine the sound of your voice?"

"I was testing a theory," she replied with a soft smile.

His brow rose. "What is a theory?"

"I once had a dream of you, and in the morning, I heard voices in an empty room. I heard *your* voice, Thomas, beckoning me to come to you. Just as I was questioning my sanity, this ring magically leapt onto my finger, causing me to fall through time. I wanted to see if I could do the same," she answered, offering him a chalice of wine. "Besides, I needed to talk to you."

"'Tis the middle of the night."

"Yes, but I couldn't sleep without discussing something with you."

"Then put me out of my agony and tell me what you wish to have speech about so I can return to my chamber. I cannot bear seeing you dressed thusly and not touch you or make you mine in every way," he murmured, his voice strained.

She had never wanted a man more than she wanted Thomas. Her earlier decision was all the more clear now that he was in her room.

"First, would you please tell me what *mo ghràdh* means?" she asked hoping Thomas felt the same as she did. He gave her that slow smile that made her insides melt.

"'Tis a Scottish endearment. The words mean *my love*."

She nodded at his admission but still wished to hear his plans for them out loud. "I want to stay with you in this time and place," Jade blurted out before she lost her nerve, "but I want to know if you feel the same way."

She held her breath, waiting for his answer.

He came to her, raising her fingertips to his lips. His mouth brushing lightly over her knuckles caused her heart to race. Her tongue licked her dry lips, and she watched his blue-gray eyes widen until a grin lit his face.

"Aye, I wish you to stay with me always, Jade. I want to ask Lord Dristan permission for us to wed if this is also what you desire."

"Are you asking me to marry you?"

"Aye, if you shall take me as your husband."

"Then, my answer is yes," she replied, while her cheeks blushed with her answer.

He took her into his arms, and she felt as if she were drowning in pleasure when his mouth descended upon hers. She wound her arms around his neck and held on, for she never wanted to let him go.

When he finally let her up for air, she stood away from him before going to one of the chairs by the fire. She turned it and sat so she was now facing him.

"I realize we hardly know one another and yet I feel in my heart I have known you all my life. This may seem sudden, but I wanted to let you know, I love you, Thomas," she declared, almost afraid he might sprint from the room.

Instead, he came to kneel before. "I love you, too, Jade, and swear to protect and care for you all of my days."

"And your nights?"

"Most assuredly, my lady."

Jade leaned forward to take his face in her hands and stare into his eyes, her thumbs caressing his cheeks. She believed with all her heart he spoke the truth and gave him a quick kiss. He seemed startled by her gesture but even more so when she lifted her hand to show him how the ring now glowed brightly. She took hold of the band and easily pulled it from her finger to offer it to him.

"I believe this belongs to you. It's only right I return it to you since the ring is what brought us together."

He smiled but still did not take what she freely offered him. "I believe 'tis the custom for the man to give a ring to his would-be bride, not the other way around," he chuckled.

"I'm certain you'll make it up to me when the time is right."

She laughed and went to put the ring upon his hand. They both gasped when the ring grew in size, and Jade gently slipped the ring onto Thomas's finger. They watched in disbelief as its glow began to fade, and the ring appeared as any other piece of jewelry, yet they knew the truth of the magic it possessed.

"Thomas," she murmured his name in a soft caress. "I think it will take the rest of the night to prove I'm not going to disappear and return to my own time."

He stood, pulling her into his arms. "Time would not be so fickle as to tear us apart now that we have found one another. Besides, I believe I owe you one last kiss afore I must needs return to my chamber."

Her eyes twinkled in merriment. This man wasn't going anywhere tonight if she had anything to say about it. "Did you know that one kiss could last for hours?"

"Can they now? I do believe, my lady, you are inviting me to stay with you this night. Is this so?" he asked with that roguish grin she had come to love.

"Thomas..." Her words left her and lingered in the air between them when he began to nibble at her ear.

"Aye, my love?"

"Go bolt the door," she ordered.

"As my lady commands." His grin this time was truly wicked. He bowed to her before doing as she asked.

Jade forgot about anything else but the man who carried her to her bed. Their lives together would begin this night, and they would forget everything else but creating a memory to last them throughout all eternity.

Jade felt the warm metal of the ring while Thomas's hand caressed her fevered skin. She sighed in contentment. The ring was where it belonged, and so was she.

Lennox Castle
Six Months Later

Laird Fergus Kincaid sank into a chair as though someone had swept his feet out from under him. He watched in disbelief as his son Thomas walked into his hall, a beautiful blonde-haired woman, far along with child, at his side. He had missed his oldest son for all these years but had not the courage to send for him to return home. Now, here he was, walking boldly into the place as though 'twere but yester eve he had last graced the land of his birth.

Fergus had no one to blame but himself for his son's absence. He could have sent a missive at any time to bring him home, and yet something he could not explain caused him to never do so. He would ask

Thomas's forgiveness for being a stubborn fool, but would do so in the privacy of his solar and not in front of the entire clan. He did, after all, have some pride left to salvage.

Thomas came afore him and knelt. "I ask your forgiveness, Father, for losing our ancestor's ring," he said aloud for all to hear.

That damn ring has cost us much, Fergus thought, even whilst he began to finally realize 'twas not the ring that had been at fault but his own lack of faith that his son would somehow return it to the clan.

"I forgive ye, Thomas, as I hope ye can forgive me," he answered, reaching out for his son.

They stood as one and clasped one another in a fierce embrace.

"My son returns home!" he called out, and those who were witness to Thomas standing proudly next to their laird began to cheer.

"I have something for you, Father," his son said.

He watched when Thomas took something from his finger and handed it to him.

'Twas the ring Thomas had lost all those years ago. "But how—"

Thomas laughed, cutting off his words. "'Tis quite the story, Father, but such a tale should be retold only to family."

"We can retire tae my solar for the telling," Fergus stated, still staring down at the ring with its guiding star.

A squeal of feminine delight sounded through the hall, causing Fergus and Thomas to turn around and look at what was the cause. "Let me introduce you to my wife, Jade. That is, if I can get her away from mother and my sisters long enough to introduce you."

Fergus took ahold of Thomas's arm. "Here," he said, holding out the ring for his son to take. "'Tis still yours, and it belongs tae ye now."

Thomas gave him a hearty slap upon his back and laughed. "You hold on to it for me, Father. It has served its purpose and brought me the love of a good woman much like you found in Mother."

Fergus watched as his son went to his wife and gave her a quick kiss afore he engulfed his mother in his arms. Fergus took in the scene and was content after so many years wishing for his son's return. He gazed down at the ring that began to glow, but that was hardly what caused his eyes to widen. For as the ring became brighter, it also became transparent afore it disappeared right afore Fergus's eyes.

He had no explanation for what he had just witnessed nor did the ring's disappearance seem to matter. His son had returned home, and his family was complete. He would not ask for more than that.

And so the ring was gone. But would it reappear again to guide other hearts that belong together somewhere in time? Perhaps. For anything is possible when your heart is searching for that special someone and for one last kiss.

BONUS MATERIAL

The following material appeared on the Bluestocking Belles' blog, the Teatime Tattler. I hope you enjoy these original pieces that continue Jade and Thomas's journey to finding love and also a glimpse into Zoe's story one day.

HER'S FOR THE TAKING

Fira stomped her foot, frustration etched its way across her face. Why, oh why, whenever she started to have feelings for a man did he turn around and give his affection to another. She stormed into Berwyck's kitchen but not before she turned back to gaze into the hall one more time.

There she was... another woman who found her way to the castle to create a buzz as several knights began vying for her attention. A lady, Fira had been told, but the stranger did not act like any lady she had ever been in service to before. Most demanded Fira's time to fulfill their every little whim. This woman had yet to ask anything of a mere serving girl.

"He is a handsome one, isna he, Fira?" One of the women in the kitchen sighed while the rest giggled.

Sir Gaillard de Rowen was indeed a man who knew how to catch a woman's eye. Did he not just yester eve hint he would like to get to know her better? "Oh, aye," Fira answered with a dreamy smile. "Gaillard makes me swoon just thinking of him."

The women broke out in laughter causing Fira to frown.

"Have ye no eyes in yer head, lass?" Cook chimed in. "We were talking about Sir Thomas."

Fira went back to the entry to the hall. Hope lingered in her heart thinking she might still have a chance. Where Sir Thomas was dark, Sir Gaillard was fair. Her attention focused on the trio across the hall. The two men were now with *Lady* Jade and Sir Thomas did not look pleased. As Fira watched the woman take Sir Thomas's hand as he led her to the raised dais, Fira's heart soared. She still had a chance with Sir Gaillard!

"I prefer the other knight," Fira finally replied.

One woman spoke up from the table as she kneaded dough. "Ye best stay clear of the likes of him, if ye know what's good for ye, Fira" she said with a smirk.

"He *is* good for me," Fira retorted, "and has been nothing but kind."

"He only wants one thing from ye," another called out, "and he can get the same from any of the whores in the village."

Fira whirled upon the group with a raised fist. "I tell ye, he does care for me!"

"Why would he settle for a serf when he can have some rich liedy?" another asked.

"The only thing Sir Gaillard is good for is eating, drinking,…"

"…and puttin' a babe in yer belly," another finished while the women once more erupted in laughter.

Fira ignored them, along with their crude comments that continued to cause laughter in the kitchen. Grabbing another pitcher of wine, she put a smile on her face and went back to serving. If she played the game well, she just might find herself wed to Sir Gaillard before the new lady at the castle realized what a catch the man really was!

HE BELONGS TO ME

Jade Calloway made her way into the Great Hall of Berwyck Castle still feeling overwhelmed by the miracle of her slipping through time. She saw Thomas standing near the massive fireplace with a group of his fellow knights. He raised a tankard of mead to his lips but paused when he saw her across the room. A smile reached his eyes and Jade blushed while she remembered their first kiss.

With a sudden urge to be near Thomas, Jade began to make her way through the hall before a serf bumped into her. Wine from the pitcher the young woman held sloshed onto Jade gown. A gasp of surprise rushed passed her lips when her garment became soaked to her skin.

"Ye best leave and return from whence ye came," the girl said through clenched teeth.

Jade's brow rose while she tried to remember the woman's name. "Fira, isn't it?"

"Aye."

"No apology for ruining my gown?" Jade asked wondering why Fira was looking like she would have no problem thrusting a dagger into Jade's back.

"He belongs to me," Fira growled out.

Jade's gaze went to Thomas who began to make his way towards her. "Who? Sir Thomas?"

"Nay... not him. Sir Gaillard. Stay away from him because he is mine." Her eyes darted about the hall before she let out a curse and fled.

"Gaillard? You can have him," Jade murmured watching Fira's departure before she felt Thomas's hand reach around her waist.

"Is she troubling you?" he whispered in her ear causing Jade to shiver with his nearness.

"No but that one is trouble, mark my words."

"She is but a woman," Thomas replied taking her arm.

"Said all men throughout time when they can't see what is right before them," Jade said with a laugh.

"Go change your gown and let us be about our day. Forget about Fira. These things have a way of working themselves out for the best," Thomas said ushering Jade to her chamber.

And with his words, Jade forgot about the angry serf who was under some impression that Jade was after Gaillard. She had better things to do with her time here in twelfth century England than worry about a jealous woman.

ZOE AND THE RING

Zoe's breath hitched. She must be dreaming. How else could she possibly be walking through an ancient hall in a medieval castle? She moved forward, or more like floated, so she knew she must have been sleeping.

She watched the scene play out before her as though she watched it on a flickering movie screen. She smiled when she saw her friend Jade conversing with a knight at the raised dais. The name Thomas skimmed across her mind and Zoe knew her friend had found her soul mate whether Jade knew it yet or not. But how was any of this possible?

A feeling of being watched washed over her and she suddenly turned as though a force beyond her control made her do so. Startled, she came face to face with a handsome stranger. A knight of olden days to make any fair maiden lose her heart in the instant their glances met. Tall with black hair that fell below his broad shoulders, the knight continued to watch her with sparkling blue eyes as though he knew some secret she was not privy to.

"*Mademoiselle*," the knight murmured before taking her hand and raising it to his lips. His eyes searched hers until they assessed her clothing... her very modern day clothing.

Zoe suddenly felt out of place. "Sir..." she allowed her unfinished words to linger in the air between them.

"Morgan... at your service," he replied. He looked around the room before he took her arm and placed it in the crook of his arm. A jolt of heat raced up her hand at the contact. "You appear lost. Mayhap you are one of the new ladies come here to attend the Lady Amiria?"

Zoe's eyes widened. "Lady Amiria? As in the lady of Berwyck Castle?"

"Is there any other who could measure up to such a name?" he chuckled. "Let me escort you to her. She will be able to ensure you are properly attired. You must have traveled a long way in order to be here."

"Sir Morgan, I need you to take me to Kenna. Is she here?" she asked quietly. Kenna would be able to explain everything... after all... the woman was her great-grandmother, several generations removed that is.

"She must still be outside. We had several men who were injured in the lists this day. Come, I can take you to her hut," Morgan said, as he began ushering Zoe from the hall.

He grabbed at a cloak thrust into his hand by a servant and placed it upon her shoulders. She shivered when he closed the clasp at her neck. "Thank you," she murmured, suddenly feeling shy in the presence of this very handsome knight.

"You are most welcome, Lady..." he gave her this lopsided grin that completely transformed his rugged face making him appear several years younger.

Zoe laughed realizing she had not given her name. "Zoe. It's a pleasure to meet you, Sir Morgan," she answered him as she thrust her hand forward for him to take.

He looked at her offering oddly before taking her hand in his calloused one. Warm heat seared straight to her heart and Zoe watched his eyes widen at their contact. He raised her hand once more towards his lips but instead kissed the inside of her wrist. Her toes curled and she swore such a sensation had never before consumed her of this magnitude.

"The pleasure is mine, dear lady. Perchance once you have concluded your business with our healer, you would allow me to accompany you to the table to break your fast."

Zoe smiled. "I would love to, kind sir," she said. *I could get used to this kind of treatment.*

He opened the door of the hall and Zoe walked outside only to stare in wonder at what she saw: snow falling upon a full-blown medieval castle in all its glory. She should have been watching where she was going but she was so preoccupied with the view and her companion that she completely missed the steps in front of her. She began to tumble forward while a scream tore from her lips.

Arms of steel wrapped around her to break her fall and her arms automatically went around his neck as though holding onto Morgan was the only thing that kept reality and her dream from colliding. His lips parted and she watched when his head began to bend forward to steal a kiss. She had never wanted anything more in her entire life.

"Zoe!"

Their lips were but a breath away. Quickly they broke apart but Zoe still clung to Morgan's arm, afraid that if she were to let go she would lose him to Time.

"Zoe... you must needs go home!" Kenna's voice rang out in the inner bailey.

Morgan pulled her close, even while Zoe knew she was beginning to return to her own place in time. "Stay with me..." he murmured against her ear. "I just found you and cannot let you leave me so easily."

Zoe reached up to cup his cheek, rubbing her thumb against his five o'clock shadow. "I would stay if I could," she whispered. "Remember me..."

"Always." He took her hand and once more placed a gentle kiss into her palm. "Come back to me, Zoe," he said before leaning forward to kiss her.

It was everything she would ever want in a first kiss and as she tightened her arms around this handsome knight she gave herself into the moment... that was until her eyes snapped open and she found herself staring up at the ceiling in her apartment. A sob tore from her throat while she flung off the covers to sit at the edge of her bed.

"Why!" she yelled out in frustration only to see a vague vision of Kenna standing before her. "Why? Why would you show me him and then not let me stay?"

"Dearest granddaughter... I showed you nothing other than what you desire but you are not finished with your work in this time and until you are, you must stay here."

"But what about Morgan?" she asked while tears ran down her face.

"You will know when it is the right time and place for you to find each other again. He will be waiting for you to come home..."

Zoe reached out for the woman who had been a constant in her life yet lived century's ago. Before her grandmother faded from view, a soft golden glow began shimmering in her hand. She blew a kiss and a twinkling trail like starlight went towards Zoe's bedside table. Zoe stared in wonder when a golden ring took shape. She reached over to clasp the ring to her chest and smiled knowing she would one day see Morgan again.

And in another place in time, Morgan awoke to still feel the lips of Zoe upon his own. He reached up to feel them still tingling from the contact. He began to dress to seek out Berwyck's healer knowing Kenna would have the answers he stood in need of. He needed to find Zoe no matter the cost. Even Time itself would not keep them apart!

Dearest Reader:

Thank you for your continued support by purchasing this novella. Originally in the box set *Follow Your Star Home: A Bluestocking Belles Collection*, I jumped at the chance to write one of my medieval/time travels for your reading pleasure. I must admit I really love writing in this genre and I hope you enjoy reading these stories as much as I love writing them.

Coming soon will be *Love Will Find You* featuring Killian of Clan MacLaren and Ella Fitzpatrick. You first met Killian in my debut novel *If My Heart Could See You* and most recently in *To Love A Scottish Laird: De Wolfe Pack Connected World*. You were first introduced to Ella in *Only For You* and also got a brief glimpse of her in *To*

Follow My Heart. Those pesky secondary characters tend to have a mind of their own but I admit I have no issue giving them their own happily-ever-after stories.

I still have several manuscripts at various stages so I'll have more coming your way. The day job still has to take priority to keep that roof over my head but my passion is still my writing. I enjoy the emails that I receive from you asking when a certain character will get their story. It makes me smile each and every time to know you are as invested in them as I am! So much writing to do... so little time. I'm sure you can understand.

I would like to thank the Bluestocking Belles for allowing me to keep the "vision" of their characters while Jade slips through time and also for their continued support. I'm happy to be associated with such an incredible group of authors.

As always, I must also thank my family for their support as I try and keep this all together. Life tends to get in the way sometimes but their understanding when I have deadlines doesn't go unnoticed. Really... I swear we'll have some sparkling conversation soon at some point.

And thank you to my loyal readers. Your patience waiting for me to write that next book means the world to me, along with the time you take to write such wonderful reviews. I continue to read them all. I am humbly grateful to each and every one of you.

All the best,
Sherry Ewing

Medieval & Time Travel Series

To Love A Scottish Laird: De Wolfe Pack Connected World

Sometimes you really can fall in love at first sight...

Lady Catherine de Wolfe knows she must find a husband before her brother chooses one for her. A tournament to celebrate the wedding of the Duke of Normandy might be her answer. She does not expect to fall for a man after just one touch. Laird Douglas MacLaren of Berwyck is invited to the tournament by the Duke of Normandy. He goes to ensure Berwyck's safety once Henry takes the throne. He does not expect to become entranced by a woman who bumps into him. Yet, nothing is ever quite that simple. Not everyone is happy with the union of this English lady and a Scottish laird. From the shores of France, to Berwyck Castle on the border between their countries, Douglas and Catherine must find their way to protect their newfound love.

If My Heart Could See You: The MacLaren's, Book One

When you're enemies, does love have a fighting chance? Amiria of Berwyck vows to protect her people by pledging her oath of fealty to the very enemy who has laid siege to her home. Dristan, the Devil's Dragon of Blackmore, has a reputation to uphold as champion knight of his king. Lies,

treachery, and deceit attempt to tear them apart, but only
love will bring them together

For All of Ever: The Knights of Berwyck, A Quest Through Time (Book One)

Sometimes to find your future, you must look to the past...
Katherine dreamed of her knight all her life yet how could
she know she'd be thrown back into the past? Nothing
prepares Riorden for the beautiful vision of a strangely clad
ghost appearing in his chamber. Centuries keep them apart
but will Time give them a chance at finding love?

Only For You: The Knights of Berwyck, A Quest Through Time (Book Two)

Sometimes it's hard to remember that true love conquers all,
only after the battle is over... Katherine has it all but settling
into her duties at Warkworth is dangerous to her well-being.
Consumed with memories of his father, Riorden must deal
with his sire's widow. Torn apart, Time becomes their enemy
while Marguerite continues her ploy to keep Riorden at her
side. With all hope lost, will Katherine & Riorden find a way
to save their marriage?

Hearts Across Time: The Knights of Berwyck (Books One & Two)

Sometimes all you need is to just believe... Hearts Across
Time is a special edition box set that combines Katherine and
Riorden's stories together from *For All of Ever* and *Only
For You.*

A Knight To Call My Own: The MacLaren's, Book Two

When your heart is broken, is love still worth the risk? Lynet of Clan MacLaren knows how it feels to love someone and not have that love returned. Ian MacGillivray has returned to Berwyck in search of a bride. Who will claim the fair Lynet? The price will be high to ensure her safety and even higher to win her love.

To Follow My Heart: The Knights of Berwyck, A Quest Through Time (Book Three)

Love is a leap. Sometimes you need to jump... Jenna Sinclair is dealing with a horrendous break up with her fiancé when she finds herself pulled through time to twelfth century England. Fletcher Monroe has spent too much time pining away for a woman who will never be his until a strangely clad woman magically appears. Torn between the past and the present, will their growing love survive a journey through Time?

The Piper's Lady in Never Too Late, A Bluestocking Belles Collection 2017

True love binds them. Deceit divides them. Will they choose love?

Lady Coira Easton spent her youth traveling with her grandfather. Now well past the age men prefer when they choose a wife, she has resigned herself to remain a maiden. But everything changes once she arrives at Berwyck Castle. She cannot resist a dashing knight who runs to her rescue, but would he give her a second look?

Garrick of Clan MacLaren can hold his own with the trained Knights of Berwyck, but as the clan's piper they would rather he play his instruments to entertain them—or lead them into battle—than to fight with a sword upon the lists. Only when he sees a lady across the training field and his heart sings for the first time does he begin to wish to be something he is not.

Will a simple misunderstanding between them threaten what they have found in one another or will they at last let love into their hearts?

One Last Kiss: The Knights of Berwyck, A Quest Through Time, Book 5

Scotland, 1182: Banished from his homeland, Thomas of Clan Kincaid lives among distant relatives, reluctantly accepting he may never return home... until the castle's healer tells him of a woman traveling across time...

Dare he believe the impossible?

Present Day, Michigan: Jade Calloway is used to being alone, and as Christmas approaches, she's skeptical when told she'll embark on an extraordinary journey. But when a ring magically appears, and she sees a ghostly man in her dreams...

Dare she believe in the possible?

Regency's

A Kiss For Charity

Young widow, Grace, Lady de Courtenay, has no idea how a close encounter with a rake at a masquerade ball would make her yearn for love again. Lord Nicholas Lacey is captivated by a lovely young woman he encounters at a masquerade. Considering the company she keeps, she might be interested in becoming his mistress. From the darkened paths of Vauxhall Gardens to a countryside estate called Hollystone Hall, Nicholas and Grace must set aside their differences in order to let love into their hearts.

The Earl Takes A Wife: A de Courtenay Novella in Valentines From Bath: a Bluestocking Belles Collection 2019

It began with a memory, etched in the heart.

Lady Celia Lacey is too young for a husband, especially man-about-town Lord Adrian de Courtenay. But when she meets him at a house party, she falls in love.

Adrian finds the appealing innocent impossible to forget, though she is barely out of the schoolroom and a relative by marriage.

His sister's deception brings them together, but destroys their happiness. Can they reach past the hurt to the love that still burns?

Nothing But Time: A Family of Worth, Book One

They will risk everything for their forbidden love...

When Lady Gwendolyn Marie Worthington is forced to marry a man old enough to be her father, she concludes love will never enter her life. Her husband is a cruel man who blames her for his own failings. Then she meets her brother's attractive business associate, and all those longings she had thought gone forever suddenly reappear.

A long-term romance holds no appeal for Neville Quinn, Earl of Drayton until an unexpected encounter with the sister of the Duke of Hartford. Still, he resists giving his heart to another woman, especially one who belongs to another man.

Chance encounters lead to intimate dinners, until Neville and Gwendolyn flee to Berwyck Castle at Scotland's border hoping beyond reason their fragile love will survive the vindictive reach of Gwendolyn's possessive husband. Before their journey is over, Gwendolyn will risk losing the only love she has ever known.

One Moment In Time: A Family of Worth, Book Two

One moment in time may be enough, if it lasts forever...

When the man Lady Roselyn Anne Winslow has loved since she was a young girl begins to court her, Roselyn thinks all her dreams have come true... until the dream turns into a nightmare.

Lady Roselyn is everything Edmond Worthington, 9th Duke of Hartford, could ask for in a wife and he is delighted to find she returns his love... until he loses her, not once but twice.

From England's ballrooms, to Berwyck Castle and a tropical island that is anything but paradise, Edmond and Roselyn face ruthless enemies who will do anything to tear them apart. Can they recover their one moment in time?

Under the Mistletoe

A new suitor seeks her hand. An old flame holds her heart. Which one will she meet under the kissing bough? When Margaret Templeton is requested to act as hostess at a Christmas party she did not think she would see the man who once held her heart. Frederick Maddock, Viscount

Beacham never forgot the young woman he had fallen in love with. Will the two finally put down their differences and once again fall in love?

You can find out more about Sherry's work on her website at www.SherryEwing.com and at online retailers.

SOCIAL MEDIA

Website: www.SherryEwing.com
Email: Sherry@SherryEwing.com
Bluestocking Belles: www.bluestockingbelles.net/
Amazon Author Page: http://amzn.to/1TrWtoy
Bookbub: www.bookbub.com/authors/sherry-ewing
Facebook: www.Facebook.com/SherryEwingAuthor
Goodreads: www.Goodreads.com/author/show/
8382315.Sherry_Ewing
Instagram: https://instagram.com/sherry.ewing
Pinterest: www.Pinterest.com/SherryLEwing
Tumblr: https://sherryewing.tumblr.com
Twitter: www.Twitter.com/Sherry_Ewing
YouTube: http://www.youtube.com/SherryEwingauthor

Sign Me Up!
Newsletter: http://bit.ly/2vGrqQM
Facebook Street Team:
www.facebook.com/groups/799623313455472/

ABOUT THE AUTHOR

Sherry Ewing picked up her first historical romance when she was a teenager and has been hooked ever since. A bestselling author, she writes historical & time travel romances to awaken the soul one heart at a time. She is a member of Romance Writers of America, the Beau Monde, and the Bluestocking Belles. Sherry is currently working on her next novel and when not writing, she can be found in the San Francisco area at her day job as an Information Technology Specialist.

You can learn more about Sherry and her published work at:
www.SherryEwing.com
Email: Sherry@SherryEwing.com